T0078038

SPIRIT
OF
FEAR

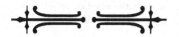

S. J. Smale

ISBN: 978-1-6987-0460-9 (sc)
ISBN: 978-1-6987-0459-3 (e)

Trafford rev. 11/18/2020

 www.trafford.com
North America & international
toll-free: 844-688-6899 (USA & Canada)
fax: 812 355 4082

Fear finds us as early as childhood.

Bogeymen hide under our beds and
monsters in our closets.

We learn early in life that parents have this
wonderful power to chase away our fears.

But when we grow older and fear sneaks up
on us we learn our parents have lost the power
they had before, and make us wonder if they
ever did hold that power in the first place.

Now life teaches us to unite as a family, to band
together in order to face the fears. We know too
that fear will never be exterminated, only beaten
down until it rears up its ugly head the next time.

My family has been blessed with the gift.
We have stared fear in the face and battled
it on our terms. We know fear takes many
forms and shapes and likes to hide.

Knowing where to look is the key.

I wish to thank my family for standing
alongside me through our many battles.

"And trust me, my dear readers, there have been many."

ONE

S tella sat at the kitchen table at the Manor. Gwen had gone through a terrible ordeal weeks ago. Once again she found herself the victim of being kidnapped by the Wizard Wilfred and his Warlock father Geoffrey. She was so angry her body shook with it. Each time it showed that she does not have the power to protect or save herself. It grated her to know that it was up to her younger sister to rescue her each and every time.

Wanda wrapped her arms around her while, Maria, Gertrude, Tempest and Morgana could only sit and watch her, unable to find the words to comfort her. Each time they tried to speak Gwen screamed at them.

Garrett was useless when it came to female emotions. He didn't think it cowardly to slink out of the room. In his mind he justified leaving them as doing the courteous thing. Besides, listening to the ear-splitting screams from Gwen was beginning to give him a headache.

Stella's heart bled for her sister. Being the target on two separate occasions and having her life threatened on both must be terrifying to her. But this tirade of hers has gone on for nearly an hour. Enough was enough. Stella slapped the table with both palms loud enough to have everyone's head spinning to look at her.

"Gwen, there is nothing any of us can say that will take away what happened to you. We are all just thankful that you came out of it alive. Now stop the bloody screaming. You know none of us saw it coming or we would have protected you." Stella threw up her hand to halt whatever scathing remarks Gwen was about to spew out at her.

"You would be the first one to fight any such protection, 'Miss I can take care of myself'," Stella threw out sarcastically. "You are safe and alive and the ones responsible will not be able to come at you again for a very, very, long time, if at all. So cool the thrusters Sis." Stella's eyes narrowed in both anger and the start of her own headache.

"The case is closed and we have Glenda Stokes charged and in custody until her trial. There is enough evidence to lock her away. Garrett and I conjured a spell that will keep her from using her powers hopefully for many years."

"Damn it all to hell Stella, I'm getting so tired of this. Don't misunderstand me, I'm not jealous, but why couldn't I have received powers that I could use to protect myself from these situations. All I can do is read minds and heal others emotions, not much there to ward off attacks." Gwenevere pouted. "I always have to rely on you to save me."

"Of course your powers can be used to protect you. If any of us thought you might be targeted again, we could have alerted you to keep your mind open for it and you would have been able to get to the safety of the Manor. But none of us dreamed he would come after you again. We didn't even know all the players until it was too late."

Gwen had to admit her sister was right. Had she seen into Geoffrey or Wilfred's mind, she would have known they were coming after her. As soon as she settled down enough to think things through more clearly a sense of fear filled her. But then she remembered that she can't read a Warlock's mind. She'd have had to keep popping in and out of Stella's in order to sense if she was in danger.

"Stella, how many are out there like you and Garrett. I thought you two were the only ones. I mean you are what you are because of the father you have. Garrett isn't mean and that's because he comes from the kindness from Gavin's side. Glenda doesn't have goodness in her."

"Yeah, we thought of that. We know that Ravena set down a law that no Warlock, without goodness in him, was to mate with a fairy, but then Gobrath never liked to follow the laws, as we've already found out. We believe she is from Gobrath's side."

"Then let us hope that she is the only deviation developed in our time from that union."

The room went silent as everyone's thoughts were the same. Stella had to get back to work. She left them all there talking over the latest development. At least it took Gwen's mind off herself now as she joined in on the discussion. But she did wonder why her sister put on a façade of not showing her fears at first. When she awoke from her drugged state, she gave the impression that everything was okay with her. Maybe this is now a delayed reaction to her ordeal.

Stella drove back to her office and began the task of going through her case files. They had mounted up since her last case. Now she pulled some out of the inbox and got busy going through them. She read through the first two and tossed them aside. She opened the third one and began reading. When she came to the part about a lost dog, she crossed her eyes and banged her head on the desk.

After a few thumps she succeeded in achieving the headache that would keep her from spewing out obscenities. "A lost dog, for God's sake, do I look like a damn dog catcher?" She was about to toss it on the pile with the other discarded files when her eyes glanced at the name on the bottom of the page showing her who the person was asking her for her help.

Was this a joke? Why would Mayor Vance Barry's son want a private detective to look for a lost dog? I know pet owners get real attached to their pets, but to hire a P.I. to look for his pet was just a little ridiculous.

Tingle.

Well there was nothing for it now since her tingle meter rang out loud and clear. She knew she had to take this seriously. Stella gathered up the other files and placed them back in her inbox and put through a call to the Mayor's office.

It took awhile to go through all the run around, but she eventually reached His Honour's private secretary. She was told that the Mayor was tied up in a meeting but would get back to her as soon as possible. Stella hung up and tapped her fingers on the desk.

She knew the Mayor and knew too that he was a man of strong convictions, down to earth and of high morals. She always respected him and was glad when he won the election.

Vance Barry was instrumental in driving down the crime rate in their city, hiring more police to protect the citizens and instrumental in creating housing for the poor and shelters for the indigent. He brought in a lot of industry to this area.

So it really did not make any sense that he would agree to his son wanting to hire her to look for a lost dog. There had to be more to this.

As she was running the oddity of this through her mind, the door to her office opened. She looked up just in time to see her favourite whirlwind dash across the office towards her.

How she could run in those pointy three inch spike heels like they were track shoes always amazed her. Debra Styles, the top fashion designer, flew across the room, her long curly blonde hair bouncing around her little pixie face, her lavender eyes sparkling with joy and her little heart shaped mouth curved up in a wide smile.

She nearly knocked Stella off the chair when she pounced at her wrapping her little arms around her in a rib cracking hug. The room filled with the sounds of her delighted giggles.

"Can't breathe," Stella hissed out against Deb's voluptuous breasts, which by the way were the only large parts of her tiny body, only made Deb giggle harder.

One final squeeze and Deb let her up for air. "Oh Stella, you will never guess what," she giggled again and then hugged her own body. "We set a date. We set a date for our wedding." Deb began to bounce around the room on those stilts her tiny little feet were in.

Between her spinning around the room and her hair bouncing around her pixie face, Stella was getting very dizzy and feared she was going to toss up her morning coffee. She had to close her eyes to settle her stomach.

Stella stood up needing to go to her and put a stop to the whirling whirlwind. She towered over her with her long lean sinewy body. Her long flaming red hair pulled back into its regular ponytail that rested well below her shoulder blades. Her bangs fell to just above perfectly arched eyebrows. Her long sea green eyes sparkled back at her best friend. It was always good to see her. She reached out and took hold of Deb's arms to stop the nauseating bouncing.

"That is wonderful news Deb. When is the big day?" keeping a firm grip on her she led her over to a chair across from her desk and pushed her down into it.

It felt so good to know that she and Deb were back to being best friends again. Just thinking how close she came to losing that friendship on the last case she worked caused her heart to miss a beat. She never wanted anything to come between them ever again. It was just too painful to think about.

At that time she and George had hurt Debra, Louise and Sam because of their damned secret. One thing she is grateful for is that Shawn Riley wasn't among those that they hurt. Once it was explained to him the reason about George's fake death and funeral, he, being a cop himself understood. Just knowing that Debra and Louise have forgiven them, Debra because of her undying love for her and Louise because of the lavish party and expensive gifts, Stella wanted to sneer. She has wondered though why she hasn't heard from Sam lately.

"We decided to have a winter wedding. Oh, and I can't wait to show you my design for my wedding dress. Oh Stella, I'm going to be the most beautiful snowflake." Deb's lavender eyes glazed over in a dreamy look.

"A snowflake," Stella could only shake her head at the fanciful mind of her friend. She is the most famous designer in the world now and if anyone could pull off a look like a human snowflake walking down the aisle, she knew Deb would be the one. But the image just would not form in her brain. She just could not envision a human snowflake. 'But then she made me look like a beautiful cloud,' she thought. Nothing was impossible for this tiny genius.

"Well, I have to tell you Deb, if anyone can do it, you can. I have no doubt you will look absolutely beautiful. I'm very happy for you."

Deb's lavender eyes filled at the compliment, threatening to spill over onto her tiny cheeks. She took out a tiny handkerchief and dabbed at them and then blew her tiny turned up nose into it.

"I want you to be my matron-of-honour Stella." She bent her head down before she added, "Um Richard wants his friend Allan Bradshaw to be his best man. I'm really sorry that he did not pick George."

Stella knew how Richard felt about her and George, and was not surprised that he picked someone else to stand with him. From the way Deb was acting she hoped that their decisions did not cause any hurt to her. She knew too that it was this friend Allan Bradshaw that tried to kill George. Now she didn't know if she likes this idea of him being in the same room as George.

It didn't help her to remember that he was under hypnosis and a poisonous drug in his system. Even so, he did attempt to kill him. Stella gave a little shudder remembering that fact. Then she turned her attention back to her friend.

"Deb I will be honoured to be your matron-of-honour, and Richard has every right to pick who he wants to stand as his best man. Don't worry about it. Just know they we are very happy for the both of you."

"Oh Stella, I don't know why Richard is so against you and George. It does hurt me because both of you are my friends. But, yes you're right he should pick who he wants. After all it is his wedding too. We've agreed to ask Louise and Dave to be in the wedding party too." That seemed to brighten her up.

Still thinking of the snowflake idea, Stella almost blurted out an idea that put a jolt of fear into her. She hoped with everything she was that Deb did not plan to have her and Louise made up to look like a couple of snowballs or even snowmen. She shuddered at the thought and kept it to herself. She knew better than to put ideas into that genius little mind.

They sat and talked wedding plans, well mostly it was Deb talking wedding plans while Stella was smart enough to just sit and nod or shake her head at the appropriate times. It just felt really good to be back to normal with each other again.

George was across town in his office doing some different talking. Cop talk. Murder never takes a long holiday. The rash of murders a few weeks ago had settled down after arresting Glenda and putting her away. That spree took its toll on his squad as well as Stella's sister. He knew she was still trying to cope with what had happened to her.

It seemed criminals were determined not to let his squad get too comfortable in the lull from then to now. Cases were coming in left and right. It gave the appearance there was a special sale on homicide over the last few days. His detectives were hip deep in them.

George sat behind his desk going over every new file his detectives have taken on with them. It took time to work a case, go over the scene, collecting interviews and evidence. It almost seemed whoever these people are that were making his squad take on back to back cases knew that overloading them would bog them down.

"Look LT. we are all carrying two new cases and that's just this week while still working on the ones from before they came in. If anymore come across our desks, we won't be able to handle them." Ron Bailey flung out.

"You don't have to tell me Ron. If this keeps up I'm going to have the Chief breathing down my neck because the Mayor will be breathing down his." George frowned at the files piled on his desk.

"Has everyone just gone crazy or what?" Sally Pride shook her head. "We've never had so many in such a short time."

"It does seem odd and this is not the cycle for a full moon as we all know that increases our load. Until we go through these files together, we won't know if it is different people responsible or a gang, serial killer or a couple of people hell bent on killing. We are going to go through each and every one of them here and now and see what turns up. We might get lucky and find a connection or pattern."

All five detectives nodded their heads in agreement. Usually they worked their own cases alone but this was beyond what was usual. This was mayhem with a touch of madness. They too felt that five, or with the LT., six heads were better than one.

As he opened the first file, all five detectives took out their notebooks and got ready to get down to some serious work. George mentally rolled up his sleeves and began reading what was in the file.

It took hours, but by the time they finished going over the last file they sat as a perfect unit. There were similarities in all the files. One fact was that all the deceased reported a family pet gone missing. They found this out from interviews from neighbours. They also found out the pet was reported missing a couple of days before the murder. Another fact and this one ensured that Brass would breathe down their necks was that the deceased were all public figures. A staff member of the victims stated that on the night of their murder their master received a phone call about the missing pets and were asked to meet up the next day.

The next day never came for them. The calls were placed in the late evening apparently to make sure the victim was home. The wife on each one was away for a few days. None of the homes showed evidence of a break-in and only the victim was killed, leaving the rest of the family's household alive. Each target arrived home late from returning from a trip or a scheduled event.

Now that the detectives could see a set pattern, they knew these murders were a deliberate target. It was agreed that they all work on one case. George handed Tom Darby the files and had him lead his team. Concentrating on one will certainly close them all once it was closed.

George dismissed his squad and watched them file out of his office. The victims ranged from a City Council member to CEO's of various companies. The media so far had not made a connection as the deaths all appeared accidental or from natural causes. It was only due to his talented squad that traces of evidence proved otherwise and had the sense to keep it under wraps from the press.

Tom selected Bob's file since it was the latest one to come in.

They all gather around Tom's desk to read over the file again. Once they were all familiar with it, Tom assigned different angles and areas for each member to delve into.

They all went back to their own desks to get started on their assignments. Now that they had a sense of direction to follow, they hunkered down to do their part with a little more enthusiasm now.

Before, they were working their own cases individually without looking into the others from their teammates. Now that the Lt, showed them that putting them together proved out a pattern and all the cases could be linked they agreed with him and were willing to work along those lines.

Thinking along these lines had them now feel that these cases could be solved and not go down the way of cold cases, something they all hated and feared.

The last case they worked on involved their boss. He put himself up for bait and because he did they solved the case. Their respect for him rose up so high.

But now that that case is solved they welcomed his input into the cases that were coming in and wanted to show him they are up to the challenge.

Tom outlined the pattern that was showing up. He delegated one to check into the missing pet angle and another to check into the reason the wives were away at the time.

It seems that each one received a phone call about their missing pets so they have to check in with the staff to verify that phone call plus the phone company for the time the calls were put through.

These are simple enough to do with warrants. Tom suggested he would get busy getting those warrants for them. They all felt better now that they have a plan of action to take.

Sally suggested she would check out the wives to get a background on them and to verify their alibis for the time of deaths.

Feeling better knowing they have a plan they all got busy doing their part.

Two

Stella sat in the luxurious office of the Mayor. Vance Barry looked every bit a politician behind his mahogany desk. His full head of thick black hair with grey wing tips at the sides gave him an air of graceful aging. She noticed he was a man that liked to keep in shape. His muscular build filled out the expensive dark blue suit very well. His flawless skin proved he took great care in his appearance. Vance graced Stella with a kindly smile.

"Miss Blake," he read from her card, "or should I say Mrs. Smale, what brings you to my office?"

"While I'm working it is still Miss Blake, your Worship." She corrected him. "I received a request from your son. He wishes to hire me to look for a lost pet. I don't usually take on such cases but I was curious."

"Timothy hired you to look for Binky?" Vance's smile faltered as he looked at her a little confused. "I had no idea. Binky is our German shepherd. He's only been missing for two days. I'm sure he just ran off to meet a lady friend, if you know what I mean, and will return. I'm sorry that Timothy has bothered you with this. I'll have a talk with him tonight, rest assured."

Stella frowned, she never ignored her tingles and she was getting one now. "Mr. Mayor, your Honour, as I said I don't usually take on cases like this. However, if I could ask a favour, I would like you to allow me to help your son." She had to think fast. "You know how attached children get to their pets. If I can locate this missing Binky, I would like to do that for him."

"Miss Blake, as you know I know of your incredible record when you held your position on the police force. I admired your dedication and many successes. This is not worthy of someone of your caliber and talent even though I do appreciate the offer." He put on his best politician's face.

"Thank you for those kind words Mr. Mayor. You are quite right, I don't take on missing pets or disgruntled spouses but something in your son's letter has me wanting to take this one on. If you are going to talk to your son, please inform him that I will be taking on this case."

Stella got up forcing Vance to rise as well. She held out her hand causing him to do the same and shook his then turned and left his office.

Stella really wasn't interested in the German shepherd. It was the tingle that interested her. She decided to go see young Timothy when he got home from school. She would beat the Mayor in talking with him first.

As with all her cases, Stella returned to her office and began a search on the Mayor and his family. It took time and she was glad her feelings about the Mayor were right. He had a few pops from his college days, but all in all no serious criminal charges on him as far as she could find and he held high morals. He was a good man.

His wife turned out to be his college sweetheart. She came from a good Christian family and there was nothing in her file to send up any warning flags for her.

Timothy was in middle school, good grades, and his records show no problems. It was like looking at the lives of the Cleavers. What the hell was the tingle about, she wondered. As far as she could see this family was on the up and up.

Stella had some time to kill before school was out so she pulled some files out and decided to go through some. It was not unusual for her to work a couple of cases at the same time. This was the best part of her work, as far as she was concerned, choosing cases to work on. She did not realize she was humming to herself as she read from the files.

Louise stood in the doorway watching her and listening to her hum. It was a rare moment to see Stella so relaxed. Louise almost hated to make a sound that would be certain to break the happy moment. But she was bursting to tell Stella the news. She reached out and opened the door again and closed it with a little force. Apparently Stella did not hear the door the first time.

The sound had Stella's head snap up and her green eyes pinning Louise where she stood. Mission accomplished. The happy little moment was gone in a split second. When she noticed who it was, she softened the look towards Louise.

Even for that fraction of time, the glare from those green eyes almost made her heart stop. What was it that made Stella react like that, she wondered? It was as though she was always on guard for some kind of danger about to attack her. Louise knew in that moment that she could never do the kind of work Stella did if it kept your nerves balled up that tight on a regular basis. It struck her that her new foster sister-in-law constantly lived on the edge.

As Louise stood there just inside the door, Stella cocked her head watching her expressions change with each line of thought, first fear, and then wonder and then a look of pity. Now why on earth would she express pity? Stella merely shrugged her shoulders.

"Hi Louise, come and sit down. What brings you here?" She watched Louise gracefully stride over and take the seat across the desk.

"You know Stella, if I ever had any doubts, they'd be gone now. You and George are simply made for each other. Neither of you know how to truly relax." Louise raised her hand to fluff her perfectly groomed blond hair.

"Hey we relax." Stella frowned. She was relaxing before Louise walked in.

"No, the only thing the two of you know how to do is work," Louise argued. "But it seems to work for you both," she smiled. "Do you have time for a little chat?"

"Yeah, just waiting for school to get out," and laughed at the surprised reaction that got out of Louise.

"Okay, you have to explain that one to me. Why are you waiting for school to get out?" She was too baffled to even attempt to form a thought to explain that in her mind.

"Nope, it's a case I'm working. Sorry but I can't divulge any info right now," her lips curved up in a smile. "So tell me what brings you to my door today Louise, without calling first once again."

Louise really wanted to know but knew Stella would not be forthcoming no matter what she said. She breathed in and heaved a sigh and resigned herself to let it go and get on with her news.

"Deb called, and guess what?" Her blue eyes sparkled.

"They set a date for this winter. She's going to be a snowflake and you and I are in the wedding party." Stella watched the bubble burst and laughed.

"Oh, she told you too." Louise frowned now that the surprise was gone.

"Sorry Louise, Deb dropped by earlier and told me the news. I'm just hoping, and don't you even mention this to her, that we are not going to be dressed like a couple of snowmen." Stella couldn't hold back the shudder that image caused.

Louise laughed at the image Stella put in her head. "No, in fact I know that she wants us to look like snow-angels. Now that you mentioned snowmen, I really don't know which one is worse." But she just couldn't stop the laugh from seeing both images in her mind.

"I mean she is a fabulous designer but there are times she does go over and above with her designs."

"Louise, you do know snow-angels have wings don't you?" Stella raised her eyebrows making them disappear behind her red bangs.

"Oh," her laughter died away. "Um, let's not mention anything about halos to her okay? Because angels are suppose to have halos too." Now Louise was very worried.

"Good plan. I've learned it's always a mistake to speak your thoughts out loud to her. It gives her ideas best left to ourselves."

"I'm beginning to learn that about her. Oh, God, Stella, we all love her but sometimes she goes into another zone, another galaxy."

"Here's another thought for you Louise unless you've already thought about it. She is the most famous designer and her wedding will be news worthy." Stella waited for that bit to sink into Louise's head.

"Oh my God, I'm going to be seen around the world dressed like an angel." The colour drained from her face.

"But we love her right?" Stella howled with laughter at the stricken look on Louise's face.

"Do we love her that much?" Fear flooded her.

"Yup, we love her that much Louise," Stella said and kept on laughing.

Stella glanced down at her watch and found it was time she got a move on to be at the Barry home before Timothy got there.

"Louise as much as I've enjoyed our little visit, I have to go to work. Why don't you give Dave a call and have him take you out to dinner tonight. That should take your mind off the wedding for a few hours. I don't mean to rush you," she got up and picked up her bag, "but I really have to leave now."

Stella helped poor Louise out of the chair and took her outside. She left her there and climbed into her car to head over to the Barry's.

Maybe it was small of her but she got a real kick out of Louise's reaction to her rushing her out of the office and the outfits they were going to be forced to wear for Deb's wedding. Knowing she wasn't the only one that feared that particular day somehow gave her some comfort. And the laughter she got out of it felt really, really good. That put her in a good mood to talk to young master Barry.

She did not have to wait long. She watched Timothy make his way down the sidewalk towards his home. Just before he made the turn to his house she climbed out of the car.

"Timothy Barry?" She strode over to stand before him.

Timothy stopped, surprised and then smiled as he recognized her from seeing her on the media.

"Miss Blake did you come here to look for Binky?" He asked hesitantly like this was too good to be true. His voice cracking a bit showing her he was on the turning point from boy to young man.

"I'm here because you asked for my help." She couldn't help smiling at his serious expression. And then she watched his face radiate with a wide smile at his luck. "Why don't we go inside and you can tell me all about Binky," she suggested.

As she swung an arm casually around his shoulders her jacket swung open and his eyes widened at the sight of her gun cradled in the shoulder holster. Normally she would have attempted to close her jacket to hide what was under it, but the look of awe on his face had her leave it open. Once inside the home however, she closed the jacket to hide her weapon. She knew mother's frowned on such things.

Timothy introduced her to his mother which was unnecessary as far as she was concerned. Stella had met Mary on numerous occasions when she was on the force. She attended police functions with her husband.

Mary looked puzzled that her son was bringing a Private Investigator into the house. Of course she knew Stella had retired from the force and started her own business. She remembered her husband was saddened at her decision to leave the force.

"Mrs. Smale, I don't understand." She wavered.

"Ma'am, I keep the name Blake while I'm working. It's nice to meet you again. Your son took it upon himself to ask for my help. Apparently you have a family pet missing." She watched Mary look to her son and back at her.

"My son hired a Private Investigator to look for our dog? I'm sorry I still don't understand. Timothy what is going on dear," she queried her son.

"Mom, Binky's never run off before. I told you and dad that something was off, something wasn't right. He's never done this before." He looked up at his mom with pleading eyes. "You and dad weren't going to do anything about it and I've searched everywhere for him. I just know something is wrong. Please mom can't Miss Blake try to find him?"

"Oh Timothy I know how much you love him, but I'm sure Miss Blake has more important things to do than chase around looking for a dog. Your dad's already told you that Binky will come back when he's ready." She looked up with apologetic eyes to Stella. "I'm so sorry we bothered you with this Miss Blake."

"Mrs. Barry, I assure you it is no trouble. Can either of you tell me about the last time you saw your dog?"

Sensing Stella was not going to let it go, Mary shrugged her shoulders and led them all into the sitting room off the foyer. When they were all seated, she called for the maid and ordered coffee for her and Stella and milk and cookies for her son.

"I'm sure you know your business better than I do Miss Blake. If you seriously want to help my son I can only be gracious enough to first thank you and give you the information you ask for."

She shook her head at her son's obvious devotion to the dog and his silliness in hiring a P.I. "I last saw him here when I left to attend a charity function Saturday afternoon. He was not here when I got back around six o'clock."

"Dad and I left early to go fishing and he was here when we left the house," Timothy volunteered.

"So the last time any of you saw him was Saturday afternoon. You were all out of the house when he went missing. Did you lock up before you left Mrs. Barry?"

"Yes and I set the alarms like I always do." Mary offered.

"Is there any way Binky could have gotten out? Maybe he slipped out when one of the maids went out? Does your staff have the alarm codes?"

"Yes of course they have the codes but it was their day off last Saturday." Now Mary looked a little worried.

"Okay, so the house was empty and you were the last to leave the house. Is that right Mrs. Barry?" Stella wrote in her notebook.

"Yes but Binky did not go outside when I left. He was still curled up sleeping in the kitchen like always."

"Who arrived home first, you or your son and husband?"

"Dad and I got home before mom." Timothy spoke up.

"And Binky was not here at that time?"

"No," he tried to fight back the tears the memory of that moment caused. "I called and he didn't answer. I searched everywhere for him. He wasn't here."

Stella got up to walk back to the front door. She opened it and bent down to inspect it. There did not appear to be a break in. She asked to see other doors leading outside. Mary took her to the patio doors leading off the living room and the back door leading off the kitchen. There were no marks on any of them. She walked around the ground floor checking windows for any sign of a break in and found nothing.

When she was back in the foyer she turned to Mary. "I would like a list of everyone with the codes and keys to this house." Then she turned to Timothy. "Timothy, I am going to look into this case and see what I can do. I cannot promise anything, but I will look into it for you. Do you understand me?"

Young Timothy squared his shoulders catching her meaning. "You think Binky was taken and that he might be dead." His voice hitched on the last word.

"I'm saying I want you to be prepared for all options." She looked down at him and laid her hand on his shoulder and squeezed.

Mary's heart was in her eyes as she draped a protective arm around her son's shoulders. "Thank you Miss Blake."

When Stella left them, her tingle meter was hitting the roof. Someone in that house knows what happened to that dog. A German shepherd would not go willingly with a stranger. It was in their very nature to tear a stranger to pieces when threatened. She would get a list of names of the staff from Mary and start digging. The only reason she didn't have Mary write them down then was the fact young Timothy was there. She didn't want him going around looking at them with suspicion and tipping them off.

Back in her office, Stella decided to go through the other files and see what else she could work on. Tomorrow she would call the Mayor's wife and get the list from her after Timothy left for school.

THREE

George left work with a headache. He walked into Stella's office to pick her up and take her home. To his surprise he found her humming to herself while reading something in front of her. He smiled watching her enjoy herself not wanting to move and break the moment.

The minute she sensed him her head turned to see him standing just inside the door smiling. God, that face sculpted by the gods framed by all that long thick glossy black hair had her mouth watering. His luscious lips curved up in a smile, she wanted to taste them knowing how sweet they are. She wanted to dive into the deep blue pool of his eyes. Suddenly heat balled up in her center and began to spread its way through her system, melting her bones as she sat looking at him.

George saw the glaze form over her long sea green eyes and raised an eyebrow as he cocked his head to the side. His hands itched to run through and grab fistfuls of her long flaming red hair. A bolt of hot lust bolted straight down to his loins as his needs grew from just looking at her. He knew they would always be this way; never getting enough of each other never truly sated leaving them always wanting more.

Sparks began to stream out of them both as he crossed the floor intending to take her here, take her now. She rose up to meet him as he crossed the last few feet to her. She wound her arms around his neck and found his mouth hot and ready against hers.

Their mouths opened, tongues danced sending them floating up. He grabbed the back of her head with one hand and got busy with the other undoing buttons to get his hands on her skin. The moment he cupped her breast her moan filled him. It was a race to shed the barriers. Sparks shot out everywhere drowning out the sounds of their clothing hitting the floor. Even the heavy thud of her holster and gun was not heard through their passions.

Stella reached down and found him silky smooth and oh so wonderfully rock hard. It sent shivered through them both. His hand travelled down her lean muscled body to cup her and drink in her scream as she flew over the first crest. His need throbbed, pulsating in her hand as she guided him in. They held for a moment to drink in the sensation and then began a slow steady thrusting in and out, in and out making her muscles tense as she climbed up again. Flames licked all around them as the speed increased with their needs. Finally when he felt she was ready to leap over he gathered himself to give one last long hard thrust and they both jumped over the edge together, filling her.

They both held on for dear life as they floated gently down to the floor. Their sweaty wet bodies sliding off leaving them lying side by side gasping for air with dry parched throats.

Stella sensed the motion of George trying to muster enough strength to summon glasses of water. She gathered enough of her own strength to lift her hand to stop him. "Not here," she wheezed out. "Just give me a minute and I'll go and get us some water."

They were alone and he locked the door before crossing the room to her. He could not understand her stubbornness in wanting to do things the human way when no one was around to see the magic. But too weak to argue he lay there and hoped he did not die of thirst before she moved.

He knew that her fuzzy brain forgot about their lovemaking causing them to float in the air and sending out shooting sparks. It was amazing how that bit of magic escaped her thought process. Conjuring up a couple of glasses of water was miniscule after that wonderful feat. He wondered if when her brain cleared she'd realize the ridiculousness of her statement.

But he was smart enough not to enlighten her of this fact at this particular moment.

Stella rolled over and crawled naked on hands and knees to the stairs, up them and down the hall to her kitchen. She was on her feet and filling two glasses when she heard him staggering in. She turned and saw his tousled black hair plastered against that incredible face. His blue eyes still held the glaze of passion in them causing her to almost spill the water she handed to him when she gazed into them. Those eyes had the heat building again in her and her eyes began to glaze over.

"My God Stella," he whispered through a parched throat. "I'm not a bloody rabbit. Give me a few minutes." But as he spoke, the look in her eyes had his blood rushing south again.

"It doesn't look like you need a few minutes to me," she gazed down at his growing need and lifted a brow.

She was shocked; stunned even, to watch his face turn pink. She didn't know why but it thrilled her to realize she brought this strong Warlock to blushing. It struck her so funny she bent over laughing so hard tears sprang into her eyes and spilled down her cheeks plopping on the floor at her feet. Then she laughed even harder when she saw her reaction caused his lust to wilt. She was on her knees now doubled over in laughter.

He didn't know what made him angrier, his embarrassment or her laughing at it. But he was angry and dumped the rest of his glass of cold water over her head. That nearly stopped the laughing, but not quite. She was down to hiccupping giggles now.

"I'm going to take a shower. You can sit there and finish your laugh fest." George took off to cool his temper under the spray of the shower.

Stella took her time getting herself under control. She thought it best to let him alone for the time being until he cooled down. She used her time going back to the office and collecting their clothes. When she walked into her bedroom he was already toweling off. Without saying a word she walked into the bathroom and got busy getting herself showered.

When she finished and walked out wrapped in a towel and saw he was already dressed and it was clear that he was still miffed. She took her time drying off and getting dressed. She knew she had better apologize to him in order for them to get past this.

"George," she walked up to him and cupped his face in her hands. "I'm sorry. I've never seen you blush before and it struck me funny and I know I should not have embarrassed you that way. Forgive me?" She rose up on her toes and brushed her lips over his in a soft kiss.

George knew deep down that it was his own bloody body betraying him that brought all this about. Feeling her lips gently against his smoothed some of his ruffled feathers. "I've never, uh, blushed before." He frowned. "Let's just forget it." His male pride was having a very hard time with what his body did to him.

"Good, forgotten. Let's go home." Stella suggested to him in order to change this particular topic of conversation. Inside, she was still doing a little happy dance but steeled her expressions so that it did not show.

Seated at the dining table in their personal palace, they ate the delicious meal and talked shop. George told her about the rash of crimes and she told him about the Mayor's son hiring her.

As soon as Stella mentioned the lost dog, he dropped his knife and fork down onto his plate. "When did this pet go missing?"

Stella's tingle meter soared through the roof at the urgency he asked the question.

"A couple of days ago. Why?" Now she laid down her cutlery and stared hard at him.

"All the crimes that have been hitting us have a missing pet as well. I need to call the Mayor." George pulled out his cell and quickly put through the call.

Stella listened while George talked to the Mayor telling him to get his family out of the house immediately and to find a place to stay. He told him he would send over a police escort and assign a twenty-four hour guard. When he hung up he called headquarters and barked out orders.

She didn't like the way he just nosed in on her case. "Do you want to let me in on what's going on?" She snapped.

"Like I said all the crimes also involve missing pets. I think the Mayor and his family is a target by what you just told me. I'm sorry that our cases are joined again, but you might just have saved the life of the Mayor's family or even the Mayor himself Stella."

She drummed her fingers on the table. He had a point and she hated that he did. She really hated that another one of her cases is mixed in with his. There was nothing she could do about it and if she wanted to see to it that the Mayor and his family were kept safe, she would just have to work alongside him again.

"This case gave me a tingle from the start and I didn't know why. Now I do. I like the Mayor George, he's a good guy. I'm still going to work my case from my end, just so you know." She frowned.

"Well it would be nice to know what has happened to all the pets. Having you work that angle might help us all in the long run and I really can't spare anyone to work that part of it right now."

"So where are the Barry's going to stay?"

"I told him to reveal that only to the escort and they will report directly to me. When I find out, I'll tell you. Darling I am sorry it seems like I'm taking over another of your cases, but we will work it together. What I know, you will know." He could see the disappointment on her face. "Can I ask the same from you?"

She knew she had no choice. This was the Mayor's life in the balance. "Yes, what I find out I'll let you know." She gave in and concentrated on the meal in front of her. Her appetite was gone but she didn't want cook thinking she didn't like it, so she got down to the job of finishing the food on her plate without tasting a bite.

After George explained the pattern the criminals formed, she decided she had better stake-out the Mayor's home that night. There was nothing she could do about George setting up his own, since it was now his case too. She insisted on going alone arguing that it was her case that alerted him and he had his men staking the house out too.

George finally agreed to remain behind seeing how his going along would undermine her pride. He knows that she knows how to take care of herself. This was one thing he could do for her. Besides, if he did show up there his squad would think he doubted their abilities to do the job.

It felt strange to see her squad, okay, her former squad, parked along the roadside with her. She had to shake it off. 'This is my job now. This is what I do,' she silently kept telling herself. Another thing that grated her was the fact she had to ask George to get the staff list for her now, but that would not be until the next day.

The only good thing about this stake-out was that she insisted that she do it without him. It was bad enough that the squad was here, she did not want their new LT. here as well. That would be a show of weakness on her part.

Stella just hoped that all the strange cars would not alert the one's bent on gaining entrance to the Mayor's home to carry out their mission. She ran over in her mind the conversation she heard George have with the Mayor. He was to tell the staff that he and his family were going out for a function and that they would not be back until very late.

It was closing on to eleven o'clock when a car was spotted driving very slowly down the street heading their way with its lights out. Stella slunk down in the seat so whoever was in the car would not see her as it passed her. She didn't have to see to know that the police stake-out did the same. They were trained for this kind of work. Hell, she trained most of them.

The dark sedan slowly passed her car and one of the cops' and turned into the Mayor's driveway. As soon as she knew it was safe, Stella sat up and watched it park close to the house. She saw a light coming from inside the house as the front door opened. She was too far away to make out who it was waiting in the doorway as two figures got out of the sedan and walked in.

As soon as the front door closed, Stella climbed out of her car. She was dressed in all black and carefully made her way on foot keeping close to the shrubbery as she drew closer to the sedan. One quick glance back told her the cops were doing the same. They recognized her car even if their boss hadn't told them she would be there. Slowly, carefully they made their way towards her. Their smiling faces told Stella they were glad to have her working with them again. She felt such relief to know they still felt this way about her and that they didn't resent her being here on their stakeout.

Tom was the first one to reach her. "Just like old times Lieutenant. How do you want to play this?"

He was giving her the lead and her heart jumped for joy at the loyalty he was displaying. Stella waited for the rest of them to be near enough to hear her since all talk had to be in hushed voices. The look on their faces told her they were happy and willing to give her point on this assignment.

Keeping her voice down to a whisper she told them to take positions at the exits. They nodded and headed out to obey. She kept Tom with her and they slowly inched their way to the front of the house. Stella used Tom's radio to keep in contact with the rest. She needed eyes on the windows to find out what was going on inside and who the two figures were talking to.

Sally spotted movement in the kitchen window and reported back that one was sitting down having a nice chat with the cook. That left the other one somewhere in the house. Until they knew exactly where they were they could not enter. After a few more minutes of waiting, Bob reported in that he had eyes on the other one wandering around in the sitting room off the front foyer.

Stella knew she could bar them from exiting but she had to be alone to do that. She told Tom she would stay on the front door and he was to go to Sally and have them both go in hot and take the one in the kitchen. She took his radio and told him to get Sally to radio her when they were about to enter.

She waited. As soon as she was alone she brought the heat in just enough to be able to cast the spell. "We are going in on three," Sally reported. Stella counted slowly to four and cast her spell.

"I call upon the power of might. I call upon what is right. Let those in not get out. Let them not be able to flee. As I will so mote it be." Stella clapped her hands over her head. The air shimmered around the building.

She radioed the others to enter giving them the location of the other person. When she heard the crashing against the front door, she stepped up to it and opened the door. She found Bob and Neal straddling a hooded figure lying on the foyer floor. Bob clamped a pair of cuffs on him. Then she looked up to find Tom and Sally walking two people towards them, both in handcuffs. It appeared that the good Mayor was going to have to hire a new cook.

Stella led them out of the house closing and locking the door after them. Bob and Neal took the suspects and walked them down the laneway to secure them in the cars. Sally and Tom stayed behind with Stella.

"I can remember a lot of times we broke down a door together. I got to tell you LT. this felt good. It was like old times again." Tom's face beamed up at hers.

"Yeah," Sally agreed. "You know Stella, as much as we like the new boss, I mean your husband," she blushed. "We really do miss you. This felt really good. To work with you again felt really good."

"Thanks guys," Stella was suddenly filled with emotions. "It felt good for me too. I've always considered each and every one of you the best there is."

"We do miss you Stella. When are you coming back?" Sally walked up and put a hand on Stella's arm. The sincerity was in her eyes almost causing Stella to waver on her decision to leave the force permanently.

"Sally, you don't know how much that means to me, but I don't think at this time that I will be coming back. My life has taken on some changes and until I can figure it all out you will have to put up with your new boss." She patted Sally's hand. "Tell you what I can do for you. Since your new LT. is my husband, you have any problems there just come see me and I'll fix it for you." She tried for a laugh.

"Hey, you may be joking, but I'll hold you to that." Tom grinned. "Well we better get these slime balls back to the station. Are you going to be in on the interrogation?"

"No, but I think I'll watch it. You guys will do the job right. I want to hear what they have to say since they are part of my on-going investigation." She hesitated. "I mean if that's okay with you?"

"No problem, like I said it's like old times." Tom and Sally smiled on their way to their cars.

FOUR

eorge stood with her in the observation room. He assigned Tom and Sally to interrogate the two suspects. Tom had one in interview room A and Sally had the other in the opposite room in interview room B. They could watch both from the observation room. The Cook was still in holding.

Stella watched the two men. Now that their faces were visible under the lights in the interrogation rooms, they looked ordinary and scared. They did not have the hardened criminal look about them. In fact, looking at both of them, they appeared to be in their mid-twenties and possessed a strong resemblance to each other. She was sure they were related in some way. This just did not add up in her mind.

"Well now Sean, why don't you tell me what you and your friend were doing in the Mayor's house tonight?" Tom slapped down a folder on the table.

Sean was a little older than the other young man in the opposite interrogation room. He sat with his arms folded over his chest. His face was set, he didn't show any emotions. "I didn't know it was against the law to visit a friend." He tossed back.

"We have your friend," Tom flipped over a page in the folder, "a Miss Granger in lock up right now and we will be talking to her soon. She's the Mayor's cook. We saw her let you and your friend in. What did you do with the family pet?"

"What pet?" Sean smirked.

"If Miss Granger is a friend of yours you would know the family pet. What did you do with it?"

"No idea what you're talking about." Sean leaned back in his chair.

"Do you make a habit of visiting your friend late at night dressed in black wearing a balaclava?" Tom banged his hands on the table making Sean jerk.

"Is there a crime in the way I dress?" Sean tried for smooth but came off a little nervous.

That statement had Tom thinking of the Middle Eastern female immigrants wearing veils to hide their faces. That goes against the Canadian custom and is making a lot of people nervous, not knowing their intent. To Canadians, masks, balaclavas and veils were only worn by criminals committing crimes. Not many stop to consider it may only be a personal religious thing.

In the other interview room 'B' Sally was getting the same attitude from her suspect. She pelted out the same questions and got the same runaround as Tom. To Stella, it seemed that although these two suspects were young, they were not going to break easy.

Something inside her told her they were on a mission and would not give in easy. Catching them inside a house they were invited to enter was going to be problematic for the case if the two detectives didn't break them. Frustration began to build in her and she saw George was feeling the same way.

Both Stella and George knew that the two could not be held in custody much longer if they didn't break. They soon realized the only chance they had was if the Mayor's cook was to spill what she knew.

They left the observation room and went down to holding where the cook was being held. One look at her determined face told them instantly that she would not give the two young men up. They knew it would be a waste of time and effort to try to break her.

Word got to them that the two Kelly brothers, at least they got that much out of them, called their lawyer. After a few hours the two suspects were released through lack of evidence in a crime.

George and Stella went home.

"Well that was a waste of effort," George brooded over his glass of wine. Stella sat beside him on the sofa staring into her glass.

Stella wondered why the Detectives didn't suggest the charge of murder to loosen their tongues. After all, the only thing they got on them was the burglary angle and that belongs to the Burglary Department. She frowned not understanding why they didn't scare the brothers with a possible murder charge.

"I don't get it," Stella kept her eyes down not wanting George to see what was going on in her head. "It was the same M.O. as your other cases, but something is not adding up. My tingle meter is never wrong." Then she looked up narrowing her eyes, "who else knew about your cases?"

"Brass, me, the squad and burglary. Why? What are you getting at?" He could hear the wheels spinning in her brain.

"You seen those two boys. Do you think they are capable of murder?"

George thought back to the way the two Kelly boys put up a brave front. He saw the nerves and knew they were scared. But they didn't have the hardened look or attitude of murderers. He guessed they were more thieves than anything else and gullible enough to go along with the Granger woman's plans to rob her boss's home.

"No I can see now that they wouldn't have the stomach for such a deed."

"The Mayor knows about your cases I bet."

"Oh, come on, Stella, the Mayor can't be in on all those crimes. I won't believe that."

"No, not the Mayor, and if I'm right, not those boys either. But if he spoke of the cases in the house, maybe the cook overheard and tried using some of the M.O. for her own plans to rob him. I'm thinking this was just a case of home-invasion robbery."

"Okay, I can see that. I'll talk to the Mayor and do a deep search on his cook. Taking out the Mayor would have hit the news and I don't think whoever is behind the murders wants that, at least for now." George felt the ball of grease melt away knowing the Mayor was not in on this. He too respected the Mayor and all the good work he's done for the city.

"It's just too bad that we can't get Miss Granger to tell us what she did to Binky." Stella sighed.

"Oh well, maybe there's a way to find out. From what you told me, young Timothy is a pretty good kid." George smiled thinking ahead to a little conversation he is going to have with the cook.

Stella shuddered but said nothing. She too liked the kid and knew that George would be very careful to do whatever he was going to do without being seen doing it.

Once the whereabouts and condition of the family pet Binky, was determined, that ended her end of the investigation. She really hoped that the cook did not kill the dog.

The next day George informed the Mayor about his staff and after a chat with the cook sent one of his men to pick up the dog from where she had it hidden. Binky was a little worse for wear and starving but happy to be reunited with his family again. George was glad Stella did not have to suffer giving young Timothy bad news about his pet. According to his squad member, Timothy thinks Stella is the best Private Investigator in the whole world.

'If only all their cases were solved so easily,' he thought. Then he got down to the real work.

It happened on rare occasions, but it was not unusual for an investigator employed by an insurance company to call her for her help. After all, they get a percentage if successful in finding the lost or stolen items. The items usually range anywhere from priceless jewelry, to pieces of art and even classified documents.

"Blake Private Investigator," Stella answered the phone.

"Miss Blake? Stella Blake?" the caller asked with a heavy British accent.

"The one and only," she smiled liking the sound of his voice. "What can I do for you?"

"Miss Blake, my name is Percival Beecham. I am an investigator employed by Lloyds of London Insurance Company. I was wondering if I might come and see you on a rather important matter."

"Sure, tell me the schedule of your flight and I'll pencil you in for later that day." She decided right there and then that since nothing in her files really interested her at the moment, she would put them on hold until she talked to this Percival Beecham.

"As it so happens, Miss Blake, I've already arrived in your country and I am registered at the Belvedere. Would two o'clock suit you?"

'Pretty sure of himself,' she thought. Now she did not know whether she liked the way he took it for granted that she would be free to see him. Damned cocky of him. Then she shrugged her shoulders. It wasn't like she was busy on a case or anything.

"Yeah, okay, I'll see you here at two o'clock." She heard him hang up. "And I always thought the British were big on manners. What, no goodbye, cheerio, ta ta?" she frowned as she hung up the phone.

She sat there drumming her fingers on the desk. Lloyds of London only insured high-end. Since she had time before her meeting, Stella decided to do a little research. Whatever the Brit wanted her help for must have made the news, she thought.

She found crime was a constant that could be relied upon. Murder and mayhem were not the sole property of any one country. There were a lot of crimes committed around the globe that were deemed newsworthy. It was a fascinating read for someone in her profession.

Stella jotted down what she considered would be in the ball park for that particular insurance company to take on. When she went over her notes she found master pieces were running just slightly ahead of jewelry. Good to know, she mused. She wondered if anyone ever thought of starting up a pool for betting on such things. Good thing there didn't seem to be one or she would have lost ten dollars having betted on jewelry, but then what did she know. To her, crime was crime and all the criminals should be locked up.

That brought her thoughts back to the case George was working. Her gut told her that the Granger woman was doing a copy cat on the crime spree. The original people behind it were still out there.

She was frowning over that when a man walked in the door. She checked her watch. Nope, not two o'clock yet. Okay the man standing just inside her office was dressed pretty much as she imagined this Percival would be dressed. He wore a black three piece suit, white shirt and sported a bow tie. He sounded like an upper class tight ass Brit on the phone.

The way he held himself stiff and was that really an umbrella hanging off his arm? When he reached up and removed his bowler hat, Stella saw his perfectly groomed hair, silver grey and cut short. He was clean shaven showing a soft pale complexion. But the voice on the phone sounded at least ten years younger than this man looked.

Stella waited for him to speak.

"Excuse me Miss," it was not the same voice she heard on the phone. "Am I addressing Miss Blake?"

Startled for a moment, she nodded. "I'm Stella Blake." She watched the relief show in his eyes.

"Oh I am so glad I caught you in. May I come in?"

"Oh, yes, yes of course. Have a seat Mr. . ."

"Bentley, ma'am," he walked towards the chair across from her desk keeping himself very erect and stiff.

She motioned him to sit which he did and placed his hat and umbrella on the desk in front of him. Stella got up to offer coffee. She came back with two cups taking hers with her to sit across from him.

"Thank you ma'am," he accepted the cup with a steady hand.

"Okay, Mr. Bentley, before we get started you can call me Stella, not ma'am. Now tell me what I can do for you?"

"Sorry ma'. . . Miss Stella," he corrected. "I really don't know quite how to put this," he reached into his vest pocket and pulled out a small folded piece of paper and handed it to her.

Stella read what was written down. The writing was shaky indicating the person doing the writing was agitated or nervous. All it said was 'it is not safe, sorry.' and signed with one name, Betty.

"Who is Betty and what does she mean by it is not safe?"

"Betty is the cook where I am employed. I have no idea what she meant by that note. It was waiting for me in my quarters two nights ago. When I went to go and see her to ask her what it was all about, she was nowhere to be found. Her things were gone as well. I decided to wait until morning and see if she returned. But she did not. I took it upon myself to ask the Master and Mistress if they knew where she had gone and found out they knew nothing about her leaving. I did not wish to worry them about the cryptic note so I did not mention or show it to them. Maybe I was wrong in doing so." Bentley cast his eyes down.

"Who are your employers Mr. Bentley?" She was getting a tingle.

"Pardon Miss, its Bentley, no Mr., just Bentley. I am the butler for Mr. and Mrs. Bertrum Wesley III." He said with great reverence, sitting straighter in his chair if that was even possible.

"Are you talking about Wesley and Carter Shipping?" Her eyebrows flew up. She knew Louise and her parents were acquainted with the Wesley's. Their name popped up a few times when they were at the same charity functions as the Davenport's.

The Wesley's had moved here about ten years ago. It had to do with something about his health problems that made them move closer to the best hospital in Canada, the Western University Hospital.

"Do you have any idea why Betty thought she was not safe in that house? They must have the best security there is. They can certainly afford it."

"The security is of course top of the line, as it should be for a family such as the Wesley's. There should be no reason she did not feel safe in the house. We are treated with the greatest respect and decorum by the Master and Mistress.

"I have done nothing but think of why she wrote that down since I found the note. It does not make any sense to me. I do know that she did seem a bit off. I guess that would be the best way to describe the way she was acting, the day before I found the note. I did not inquire in case it was of a personal nature. Now I wish I had." He cast worried eyes at Stella.

"Miss Stella, I think something must be terribly wrong. I came here to ask you for your help. I was hoping that you could find her and find out what has frightened her."

Stella began writing in her notebook. She questioned him for another twenty minutes and then assured him she would look into it for him. Having her agree to take on the case seemed to ease his worry just a little. He left the office walking away as stiffly as he walked in. She assumed it was his nature or maybe years of training. As she watched him cross the street to his car, she wondered why all butlers walked like they were holding in a demanding bowel movement or had a rod jacked up their asses. She shook her head and began the task of putting the case in order from her notes.

Just as she placed the last bit of information on the crime board she set up for it, the door opened. As soon as she glanced at the man making his way in she instinctively knew it was Percival Beecham. He was dressed like a true old time Englishman from his bowler hat, his pinstriped suit, right down to the umbrella dangling from his arm. He screamed Lloyds of London.

"Please take a seat Mr. Beecham," she gestured to the chair as she took her own.

"Thank you Miss Blake," he sat and like Bentley, he placed his hat and umbrella on the desk in front of him.

"Now Mr. Beecham, what brings Lloyds of London to our shores and particularly to my doorstep?" Small of her she knew, but bad phone manners did not warrant an offer of coffee, or at least not just yet.

He stared at the tall lean redhead across from him. Her long green eyes, he noticed were very sharp. He only hoped that she would hold up to her reputation. He had no idea she took offense to his abrupt ending of their telephone conversation. All British subjects took their behavior from their Royal Monarchs. They never offered a hello or issued goodbyes. It simply has to do with time management, preventing any waste in that area. There was never any offense meant by that protocol.

When his investigation kept hitting dead ends and went cold, he was given no other option but to search for someone to help him. His wide search found her and her record on the police force. She had the highest success rate and going through some of her files, which he hacked, noticed that some had next to nothing to go on. Well his case has the same amount as of today. He was banking on her doing whatever it is she does to uncover the truth with barely a scrap of evidence to go on.

She watched him sizing her up as she waited for his answer and kept her smirk hidden.

"As you know Miss Blake, Lloyds of London insure only high-end and very valuable merchandise all over the world. In the last six months the company has been hit with over a dozen claims of burglary from as many countries. You can understand how this can be very disturbing."

"And costly," she interrupted.

"Yes, Miss Blake, it is very costly to the company to pay out the insurance money if the merchandize cannot be found and returned." He agreed stiffly.

"Mr. Beecham are you telling me that you are unable to find the perpetrators or the merchandise?"

His face grew red with heated embarrassment and anger.

"I know how to do my job Miss Blake," he snapped.

"Then why did you call me?" Oh she was enjoying this.

Stella thought his head would explode at any moment and decided she should cool down her aggravation towards him before he keeled over with a heart attack.

"Would you like some coffee Mr. Beecham? I'm afraid I don't have tea in my office." She got up to get it before he had a chance to answer. Walking away from him might give him a chance to cool off and settle down. God that's all she needed, to have him die on her in her office.

It worked. The colour in his face was fading a bit going back to its normal pale complexion. She set the cup down in front of him and went back to take her seat.

She leaned back in her chair and waited for him to collect himself enough to speak.

"As I was saying before, we have had a rash of burglaries and they have been conducted by professionals. I have not been able to find one piece of evidence. The merchandise taken is always very, very expensive jewelry. None of the gems have shown up on the market as of yet. We believe they may have been re-cut and sold off as smaller stones." He stopped to take a sip of the coffee.

"As I said before, I do know how to do my job. However, this bunch of criminals is very good at theirs. Almost like they have an inside track of how law enforcement works. The forensic side of it anyway."

That statement had her head snap up. She just finished a case not that long ago that dealt with inside help. But she was sure magic was not involved this time.

"But why come to me with this if there is no evidence for you to go on? What makes you think I could find the perpetrators if you can't."

"The company is, shall we say, most anxious to find the gems. They have instructed me to seek out help. I checked around and found you. Your records show you have an uncanny ability to solve crimes with very little if any evidence. I am asking for your assistance in this matter."

His hand gripped his cup harder at his last statement. It was and still is a blow to his pride that he was ordered to bring someone else in to work the case with him.

"I see," she swiveled back and forth in her chair. "I also did a little digging and found out that you are very good at your job too." It didn't hurt her to throw a bone his way since he had to admit to needing help, and she saw how much that grated on him.

"Okay, Mr. Beecham, I'll help you out. No guarantees, but if we are successful I'll expect fifteen percent of your take when it's finished. Agreed?" She watched the mixed emotions fly over his face. First the pent up anger, residual embarrassment and finally relief.

Stella could not help but laugh. She was saved from his outrage at her reaction by the office door opening. In walked her part-time assistant Clark Kent. She looked at her watch and noticed that it was indeed past time for school to be out.

Clark was enrolled in the local college majoring in journalism and media reporting. He admired the way Stella Blake's mind looked at facts and organized them in order to get a clear picture. He came to her earlier asking to be her assistant and to observe her in action.

At the time, Stella was skeptical but to his joy gave in and took him on, on a part time bases. He only had to promise not to miss any of his classes at school.

She acknowledged his greeting with a short wave and stood up putting out her hand to Percival. He reluctantly shook her hand picked up his hat and umbrella.

"I assume you have all your notes at the hotel?" she asked him.

"Yes, I brought everything about this case with me."

"Then we will meet in your hotel room tomorrow at oh, let's say around one o'clock. We'll go over everything you have then."

"Until then Miss Blake," Percival placed his hat on his head, tipping it slightly up and down in a gentlemanly salute holding his umbrella like a walking stick and primly walked out of the office without looking back.

"Brrr," Clark said as he pretended to shiver. "You may want to wear something warm when you go for your meeting with him tomorrow."

Stella chuckled and rumpled his hair on her way back to her desk.

"Hey is that the case on the board?" Clark's eyes lit up with excitement to see she was indeed working a case.

"It's a case, but not his," his observation brought her mind back to the Bentley case.

"Man, how do you do it? How can you work two cases at the same time? It's like mental multi-tasking." His whole face lit up in awe and wonder at her talent.

She turned to look at him and his expression brought out a laugh. Maybe having him around wasn't such a bad idea after all, she thought. Right now he reminded her of a freckle faced little puppy quivering for a treat. It would not surprise her in the least if he stuck out his tongue and started panting. That image alone had her howling.

"God, Clark it doesn't take much to make you happy does it?"

"Hey, I saw some of what you did when working only one case. Taking on two at the same time is sending me over the moon. I'm a simple person Stella," he grinned.

"You are also brilliant according to your school records. Simple or not Clark, I am proud of your hard work there." She grinned back at him.

"How do you know about my school records? We never talk about my classes." He looked puzzled.

"You think I would allow anyone to work for me, even part time, without checking into them? Come on Clark you are smarter than that I hope."

"But school records are confidential. No way would the college give you that information. We are not related. Only parents or guardians are privy to that."

"Stella Blake, Private Investigator," was all she said.

His eyes went as large as saucers, almost swallowing up his face. "Wow," was all he could think.

"Okay now, did you come in today to socialize or to work?"

"Work."

"As you can see," she pointed to the board. "We have a missing cook. Before she went missing she wrote a note to the butler stating she did not feel safe. We need to find her."

"Wow," Clark got up from his table to walk over to the crime board. "Look who she works for. I mean the Wesley's are rich, not just rich but mega-rich."

"You know about Wesley and Carter?" Her eyebrows winged up under her bangs.

"Yeah, they are in the top five shipping companies. There was a piece done on Mr. Wesley a while back. It had something to do about him having to move here for health reasons." He saw the surprise on her face. "Remember journalism, what I am majoring in?"

"Right, okay. Well, like I said, we need to find Betty Vanhorn, the cook." His reminder to her gave her an idea. "Your job is to gather all the information you can on the Wesley's, both husband and wife. I'm going to interview the other staff members and find out if they know anything."

Stella had got a list of the names of the staff and their scheduled days off from Bentley. She did not know why, but something in her gut told her not to let the Wesley's know she was looking into the disappearance of their cook.

Her tingles were never wrong.

As it happened it was the upstairs maid's day off. Stella did a search and found her address. She threw on her jacket to hide her weapon, grabbed her bag and headed out. Stella is still naïve enough to think that luck plays a part in her work.

FIVE

Deb did not leave her much time, but Louise was determined to put on a bridal shower for her. She flew into a flurry making phone calls and enlisting help. Angela was only too willing to lend her organizational skills. Gwen was thrilled to have something to do to take her mind off her trauma. She told Louise that she would talk to her family and was sure they would love to pitch in.

Louise asked them to all meet her for lunch at the Belvedere and talk over the plans over a light meal. That killed two birds with one meeting. She would get there early and talk to the manager about renting one of the ballrooms for the event. The one fly in the ointment was that she couldn't reach Stella to ask her to join them.

That brought a frown to her lovely face as she thought seriously about wearing an armored vest when she was able to catch up with her to tell her about the plans.

Sneaking up on Stella was getting to be very hazardous. Her body involuntarily shuddered thinking about that gun she carries and knowing firsthand what it felt like having it pointing at her.

At the same time Louise was doing what she is good at, Stella was too. She pulled up in front of a small house located on the other side of the tracks in the north part of the city. It looked like a little cottage with its green tiled roof and white clapboard frame. The windows were clean as a penny in stark contrast to the other homes that took up residence there.

It was a low income section of town, but Stella appreciated the way Mary Duncan took care of her tiny one-story home. It was brightened up by colourful smiling faced flowers bringing joy and welcome to the front. The lawn, although small was green and proudly trimmed. Unlike her neighbours whose were dotted with patches of brown making them look either sickly or hit by blight.

There was a little statue of mother and child placed in the center guarding the sweet little home. The green shutters, matching the roof, framed the windows, dressing the house and giving it the feeling of being loved and tended.

Stella walked up to the front door and knocked. A young woman holding a baby answered the door. She smiled sweetly as she looked up into Stella's green eyes.

"May I help you?" She rocked as she stood, bouncing the infant gently against her small chest.

"Mary Duncan?" Stella smiled down at her.

"Yes, I'm Mary Duncan. I'm sorry, do I know you?" She looked puzzled but kept the smile in place.

Stella shook her head. "Ms. Duncan, my name is Stella Blake. I'd like to ask you a couple of question." Stella brought out her I.D. and showed her. She watched the smile falter as she took a step back.

She tightened her hold on the baby which was sound asleep on her shoulder. "I don't understand. Why would a private investigator want to ask me questions?" She was suddenly terrified that she was here to take her child from her.

"Ms. Duncan I would like to ask you about Betty Vanhorn. May I come in?" Stella advanced not giving the woman a chance to deny her entrance or time to shut the door on her. Mary had no choice now but to back up and allow this tall lean woman into her home. Stella was sorry for the fear this action put in her eyes.

Stella shut the door behind her and waited for Mary to lead them to a place they could talk comfortably.

Stella tried to keep her voice calm so as not to wake the infant or put more fear into Mary. "Ms. Duncan you are acquainted with Betty Vanhorn, the cook for your employer. Can you tell me about the last time you saw her?"

"Miss Blake, I know Betty could not have done anything wrong. Why are you asking questions about her?" A bit of anger was mixed in with her fear now. Her loyalty was showing. But she was a bit relieved to know that this woman was not here about her child. She would die to protect and keep her precious baby.

"I'm not here because she did anything wrong. I'm here because she is missing and I am trying to find her."

"Oh, oh, I'm sorry I was rude to you." Mary's face reddened. "I thought you were here to take my baby from me. I'm a good mother." Mary told her.

"You were not rude to me. You have every right to be concerned when a stranger calls and wishes to speak to you. I assure you that I'm not here for any other reason but to find Mrs. Vanhorn. How old is the baby?" Stella tried to relax her by playing to her motherly instincts.

"Josh is six months old and such a good baby," she cooed and stroked her son's pudgy cheek. "Josh's father is in the army and stationed abroad. We plan to marry when he comes home." She explained. "Just let me put him down and I'll make us some coffee."

Stella watched her walk away with the baby. The little sitting room was tiny just like the house. It was spotlessly clean and sparse, but what few items it boasted were tended to with loving care. Not a speck of dust anywhere. This woman was a born nurturer and homemaker by nature she thought. Now she understood why she took up the profession of a maid. She has a natural talent for housekeeping and by all appearances a good mother as well.

After talking with Mary, she got no further information than Bentley gave her. However she did get her to swear not to discuss their conversation with her employers or other staff members. That took some persuasion but she finally got her to give her word. Stella sensed that once Mary gave her word she kept it. She did wonder how this woman happens to have a child and raising it on her own for now on a maid's salary. Not only is she a good maid and mother but it seems she is also good at budgeting. This sweet young woman should be commended for her many talents and strength.

The other staff members were on duty today, so she would have to wait until their days off to question them. Although she tried calling Betty at her home and received no answer, she decided to drive over to her house and try again, in person.

Betty Vanhorn lived in the east part of the city, but not in the more affluent well-to-do part. Her home was nestled in a tiny suburb. It was a step up from Mary Duncan's section. She pulled up outside the duplex and noted that Betty was not inclined to the same kind of pride in her home's appearance as the upstairs maid.

The windows weren't filthy but they could do with a wash and there were no freshly painted shutters adorning them. The front lawn was larger and cried out for a trimming. Weeds were allowed to choke the grass. There was no statue guarding this home. Stella began to wonder about the pay grade in that employment.

She sat in her car watching the house for a minute. As far as she could tell it looked like no one was home. As she sat watching she turned her gaze to the neighbours homes and noticed a couple of curtains move and new she was being watched. That could be very helpful, she thought.

She climbed out of the car and walked up the cracked sidewalk to the front door. She noticed that there were no sunny smiling flowers gracing the house, only shrubs which also needed a bit of trimming. Her research told her that Betty was a widow and had been for fifteen years.

She knocked and listened while she waited. She heard muffled footsteps coming from inside and knew she was being watched through the Judas peep hole. The door did not open. No one called out to her from inside. This was one very scared person.

"Mrs. Vanhorn, my name is Stella Blake. I only want to talk to you." Stella raised her voice enough so whoever was behind the door could hear her. "I am a Private Investigator. Mr. Bentley came to me. He's very worried about you." She tried to appeal to her softer side.

Still no answer.

"Mrs. Vanhorn, if you are in any trouble at all I can help you."

No answer.

"I'm going to leave my card here. Please call me. I feel you are frightened. I can help." Stella took out a card and slid it in the crack of the door and walked away.

As she drove away she looked in the rear view mirror and saw the door open and a hand come out to pick up the card that fell down onto the doorstep. Then the door closed.

Well Betty Vanhorn was alive but very, very scared.

Stella put a call in to George. Yes she was wealthy beyond belief on her own, but she was never raised with a house full of servants for good reason, only Maria. She did not know the working protocol of the domestic help.

"Homicide, Lieutenant Smale," His voice was enough to make her mouth water.

"George, I need your expertise." She didn't realize her voice turned husky with need.

George heard it, smiled as his own needs went into action from the sound of it. Not an unpleasant feeling but inconvenient at the moment. "And what part of my expertise do you need?"

She heard the laughter in his voice and frowned.

She shrugged off the aggravation she felt at his laughter and got down to business. "You have a whack load of servants, which I never see except the Butler and Cook and a couple of server. But that's something we'll discuss later. Who answers the phone when it rings?"

The question threw him for a minute. It was unusual for her to ask anything about their domestic help. "Graves answers the phone. Why?"

Graves is his Butler. "Do any of the other's answer it?"

"No Stella that is one part of his duties. Why are you asking?"

"Thanks, tell you later, got to go." She hung up on him. She didn't know why talking about his servants made her teeth itch, but it did. That had her thinking of flossy them and then instantly tossed that thought away.

Clark was busy at his table when she walked into her office. He looked up at the sound of the door opening. He marveled at her as her long strides ate up the floor as she made her way to her desk.

She looked like a warrior readying for battle. Her muscles flexed under her long lean frame. Her sharp, green eyes narrowed in purpose as she moved by him. He caught her scent as she rushed past him. It was subtle and yet hinted at intoxicating and smelled very expensive.

"I finished the search on the Wesley's' Stella." Clark's voice cracked a bit. "Bertrum was born and educated in England. Other than being born with a silver spoon in his mouth, he had a normal childhood for a rich kid. Private schooling as one would assume. He was an average student according to his records. His father owned the shipping company and handed it down to him. The recession hit them hard and he had to take on a partner, hence Wesley and Carter. Bertrum met his wife while attending college and married after his graduation.

She was born into the lower class and her parents worked two jobs each to afford her education. She was top of her class in grades. She checks out as normal too. Sorry Stella but there is nothing hinky about her unless you consider a few college pranks she apparently instigated noteworthy."

"Did you get a list of any close friends either of them had in school? If they had any, are they still in contact with any of them?" She shot across to him while updating her notebook and board.

"Well we all make friends in school. I never thought to list them down. I mean I know after I graduate I'll be concentrating on my career and figured we'd just drift apart over time. You know life taking over and all that."

He saw her head whip around and her eyes pin him where he sat. He swallowed hard. "I'll go back in and check on that list now." He turned back to his computer.

"You do that." She tossed out.

Stella sat down at her desk now and put the call in to Bentley.

"Wesley's residence," Bentley's voice sounded droll.

"Bentley, its Stella Blake. Are you alone? Is anyone around that might overhear you?"

"No one is around Miss Blake. I am free to speak. Did you find her?" She heard the concern in his voice now.

"Yes I found her and you were right to come to me. I feel something is very, very wrong. She is frightened right down to the bone and I think it has something to do with your employers."

"Oh, but Miss Blake, that cannot be. They are the epitome of decent people. I have not seen or heard of anything from them that would besmirch their good reputation. I have been in their employee for many, many years. They are fair and considerate employers. I simply cannot understand what would make her feel frightened of them."

"That's what I am going to find out. I want you to keep your ears open to any conversation they have in person or over the phone. Can you do that for me?"

"Miss, I cannot spy on them and eavesdropping is a disloyalty I would rather not be party too. My loyalty is first and foremost to my employers."

Stella could just see his back stiffen as he spoke. It was good to know that there were some people in this world that held loyalty to a high standard. But loyalty was not what was going to help the cook right now.

"Look Bentley, you came to me for help. I am telling you right now that something went on in that house that has your cook scared right down to her knee high stockings. I need you to do this for me and I can promise you that whatever you tell me will be held in the strictest confidence. You will have to unbend enough to do this if you want to help Betty."

Stella waited for him to speak. She knew he was warring with himself, torn between his loyalty to his employers and helping his friend. She heard the quiet sigh and knew he had come to a decision. This was hard for him she knew. His years of training and dedication to his trade and keeping up his standards were about to be dented.

"Very well Miss, but I will state that I find this very distasteful to say the least. However I do not wish to add to Mrs. Vanhorn's troubled state."

Troubled state, Stella huffed. Now there's an understatement. God where did they get these tight-assed Butlers? Betty Vanhorn wasn't troubled. She was scared for her life.

"Fine, good, just keep your ears and eyes open." She hung up on the little snob. "God help Graves if he ever pulled that kind of attitude around me," she growled as she banged her forehead on the desk to relieve some of her pent up anger.

"Uh, Stella are you okay?" Clark squeaked out.

"What?" She looked up. "Yeah, yeah I'm just freaking fine. Don't' ever hire a butler with a rod up his ass." She rubbed her forehead happy to feel the pain caused by the contact with her desk.

"Sure, um, no problem. Besides I don't think I'll ever be able to afford one in any case. "You mentioned a guy named Graves. Do you want me to check him out too?"

"Graves?" It took a minute to sink in and then she laughed. "No you don't need to check on him. He's not part of this. Did you get a list of the friends?" She felt better and threw him a smile.

"Ah, yeah it's being printed out right now." He waited for the printer to finish then took the sheet of paper over to her desk.

"Thanks," she said taking the paper from him. A quick scan had her eyes narrowing. She took out her marker and underlined three of the names. "Who are these friends of?" She asked Clark without looking up.

Clark leaned over and read the names. "Those are friends of Mrs. Wesley. Why? How are they involved?" His journalism was showing.

"Do you know how to say jackpot Clark?"

"Sure, why?"

"Because I think you just hit it. Back off and give me a minute here." She tapped her fingers on the desk. Should she call George or take this information and run with it herself. They were part of her investigation after all. But they were also part of George's. She knew she would have to tell George, but she didn't have to do that this instant. She did wonder why the squad didn't check into the victims' life and family lives? If they had they would have found the list of the widows' friends. That should have been their first course of action.

Stella reached for the phone.

"Wesley residence," Bentley answered the phone.

"Bentley, can you get away. I need you here. I have some questions for you." Her green eyes sparked through the feral look on her face.

"As it happens I was on my way out to pick up the dry cleaning for the Master. I can be at your office in half an hour." He hung up.

Stella got up and put the three names on the board drawing a line from them to Mrs. Wesley.

Clark watched her writing on the board. He knew that the information he dug up for her has something to do with this new bit of information on the case. What he didn't know was how it tied in. This is what he came to her to learn. It's all about her thought process and strategies. Learning these things will help him be a better reporter. Hearing that she called this Bentley guy in to her office has him excited to find out what she will be asking him.

It did bother him to know that she left the office without telling him where she was going. He came to her to learn and that requires that she keep him in the loop so he can see the way she arranges her facts and actions.

All he wants from her is to find a way to put all facts together in the right order to come to conclusions that add up. School books and professors can only teach the basics of journalism. It's the thought process to put all the facts in the right order that he needs to learn and they can't teach that. Stella is the best at this. From his research on her, she solved cases with little to no evidence or facts. Now he's watched her work multiple cases at a time and kept them all separate. That's another lesson not taught in the classroom. But he needs for her to keep him in the loop in order to learn these valuable lessons.

Six

Bentley arrived in exactly half an hour as he stated. Punctuality was ingrained in this man, Stella mused as she watched him walk in. She gestured to him to take a seat and got up from hers to fix a cup of coffee for him.

"Miss Blake, I do not like all this cloak and dagger business. I particularly do not like what you have asked me to do." He sat stiffly in his seat.

"Part of my business involves cloak and dagger as you call it Bentley. You came to me for help and this is the way I work when the need calls for it." She retorted.

God she would love to take some of the starch out of his stuffing. But then she remembered how worried he looked about the cook when he first came to her and decided to ease up a bit.

"I told you I located Betty Vanhorn. She is terrified and it has something to do with the Wesley's. I do appreciate the difficulty you are going through doing as I ask, but something is going on there that is making Mrs. Vanhorn fear for her very life. I need you to give me a sense of the schedules of your employers."

Speaking of his employers to anyone went against his grain. Loyalty was the very essence of his profession. It was a requirement that was first and foremost and to be taken very seriously. To be otherwise was very unsettling to him. But when he thought of the note and the way cook was acting before she went missing had him bending enough to do as this woman asked. Now that he was told she feared for her life, he saw no other option opened to him.

"Mr. Wesley works all week at his office. He attends a variety of charity functions, at least one a month with Mrs. Wesley. He plays golf regularly on Saturdays and enjoys a quiet day at home on Sunday. Mrs. Wesley chairs for a few charities and has a weekly lunch date with friends of hers'. She makes out the weekly schedule for meals and housekeeping. They are very kind and generous employers Miss Blake." His loyalty peeked through.

Stella showed him her list of names. "Do you recognize any of these names?"

When he glanced at the names his face paled. Being a Butler did not necessarily mean he was stupid. He read the paper and saw that a couple of the names on it were the wives of men that had passed recently. They were friends of the Wesley's and the women who lunched with Mrs. Wesley.

Stella noted his reaction to the names on the list.

"The Wesley's have attended the funerals of a couple of the husbands to the women on that list. They are the friends Mrs. Wesley has her weekly luncheon with." He looked up at her with worried eyes. "Are you telling me that the husbands of this group are targeted for harm? Is Mr. Wesley in danger?"

"When is Mrs. Wesley scheduled to have the next luncheon date?" She kept her voice calm but her eyes were hard.

"Why, it was today Miss. She just returned before you called me." Panic showed through the beads of sweat forming on his upper lip.

Stella was glad that she didn't show him the shortened list she culled from the one Clark handed her, but the full list. She picked up a marker from the desk and handed it to him.

"I need you to check the names of the women on this list that you know attend the luncheon." She watched as he took the marker in a shaky hand. His eyes were filled with fear as they stared at her before looking back down at the sheet of paper.

When he was done he handed the paper and the marker back. Stella noted he marked all but four. That still left a large number on the list that liked to meet for lunch.

"You did not answer my question Miss Blake. Is Mr. Wesley in danger?"

It must have been his years of training and working in his profession that gave him the ability to appear cool and calm when she knew he was scared to the bones. She was beginning to admire that in him. Clearly Bentley felt strongly towards his employer.

"All I can tell you now is that I think it a strong possibility."

"Then I must warn Mr. Wesley at once so he can take precautions. He is recovering from a serious health issue. His physician says he's improving greatly but I don't know what a strain on him would do? Telling him about the danger might cause him to relapse. Miss Blake what should I do?" He was hyper-ventilating and speaking fast.

"You will do nothing Bentley." She held up her hand to stop him from arguing. "All I want you to do is to watch and listen. Now that you know the seriousness of the situation I don't think doing this will go against your nature. You will do this to protect your employer."

"I see, yes, yes I will do that. I assure you I will be very vigilant in this. Before when you asked, I thought it was eavesdropping and that is very distasteful to me, and should never be condoned in a position such as mine. But to do so, in order to keep them safe is another matter altogether. Rest assured Miss Blake I will let nothing get past me."

"Good to hear Bentley. You have to agree not to tell anyone in the house about this. No one Bentley until I find out what is going on. Agreed?"

"Yes Miss Blake, you can count on me." He checked his pocket watch. "I had better be heading back or Mrs. Wesley will wonder what has taken me so long. I will claim slow traffic if I'm questioned about my tardiness."

"One more thing Bentley," he had just reached the door and turned to look at her. "Does anyone know about the note or the reason the cook has not returned?"

"No, but I am afraid I told Mrs. Wesley I heard from her and that she stated she was not feeling well and asked to take a few days leave. She questioned me later about her whereabouts when I mentioned she didn't show up for work. I hope that was alright." Bentley was clearly nervous.

"How did Mrs. Wesley take the news?"

"To be honest, she looked a little put out over the fact she would have to get a replacement. Other than that, she seemed to accept my excuse for the cook's sudden disappearance."

"Good, then you did the right thing. You better get going before you are missed. Thank you Bentley."

"You are welcome Miss Blake," Bentley nodded his head, opened the door and walked out.

After Bentley left, Stella glanced at the paper with the list of women and her thoughts went to a particular movie she saw years ago, and wondered.

"Clark, I want you to do another deep search on Mrs. Wesley and the women marked on this list." There had to be something to these women, her gut was screaming and her tingle meter went through the roof. She was going to take one more pass at Betty and see if she could get her to talk.

George was in his office going over the files again. Something was being missed. It did not feel like a leak in the 'house' this time. He decided to go through all the files one by one and note down the little details. It wasn't unusual for the small things to get overlooked. His squad was the best, but even the best were capable of missing something from time to time.

He began with the names of the victims to see if they knew each other, met each other somewhere, or did some business, attended sports or functions. When he got into it, it started to look like a list of who's who. Of course he recognized most of the names from some charity functions he attended as well. That made him wonder if he was a target as well, but he and Stella did not own a pet and that was the one common denominator to them all.

It struck him odd that there was no sign of a break in. That meant the perpetrator had access to keys and alarm codes, or inside help. When each victim was killed, the spouse was away on a trip with a solid alibi, another similarity, and it was the servants' night off. Except for one, he noticed. A downstairs maid stayed in claiming she had the flu and was taking medicine for it that had her sleeping. She claimed she did not hear anything that night.

His detectives checked with her doctor and found out she was telling the truth. She had seen the doctor the day before and was prescribed medication that would indeed induce drowsiness. And since the other murders did not have any staff on the premises, he was tempted to believe her.

All the staff from each crime scene claimed they did not give out the codes or passkey to anyone. That placed him back at square one and that was damned frustrating. It had to be someone familiar with the family or someone with expert burglary skills and knowledgeable of police forensics. That was a wide scope to cover.

George decided it was time to talk to Shawn Riley again. He was Captain of the Burglary division and he had gotten to know him better when their cases crossed earlier in the year. Also he was the one that Stella chose to walk her down the aisle on their wedding day. He might point him to someone skilled in the art of burglary with a penchant for murder.

Everyone was busy doing their own thing. Stella was concentrating on a group of women who like to gather for a weekly luncheon, George figuring out the best way to narrow down his search, and Louise was busy with her insatiable appetite for planning events.

Lauren Wesley sat in her dressing room sitting at her vanity absently preening herself as she gazed at her reflection in the mirror. Her thoughts were back at the restaurant and the happy conversation they all enjoyed.

It was marvelous; it was working like a charm. But didn't she tell them that it would work? Silly Cybil with all her doubts and fretting. How could she not see the plan was perfect? The cops were going around chasing their tales, while they all carried on with their normal routine, well, except for this one deviation from them.

They deserved to have the life they were now accustomed to. Doing things this way would ensure they reached that goal and no one could ever take it away from them. Growing up in poverty or near to it simply was not a life worthy of any of them. Somehow they all managed to marry well and soon blended in to the life-style they should have been born into, in the first place.

She thought back to the first time she and her friends had all met for lunch, each one keeping up the masquerade of the entitled. It wasn't until their third time of getting together that little slips were made from a couple letting their true upbringings peek through. Once that was revealed they became closer friends and made arrangements to meet once a week in order to shed the cloak of lies and let them be themselves for even a short time.

"And God didn't that feel good," she thought. To be able to peel off the pretense of being born into the rich and famous for just a few hours felt so freeing to them all. It was like stripping off a tight girdle to be able to breathe again.

Months later it was discovered that Bianca informed them that she suspected her husband of cheating on her. She feared it could only be a matter of time before he asked for a divorce. She was so afraid that she would be left with nothing and forced to go back to living the way she did before he married her. All the women sympathized and at the same time realized that that could also be their fate as well.

As much as they all looked the part and acted the part of the high society, their husbands knew of their upbringing and may get tired of them and want to be with someone born to their own class of people. It was a possibility that they could not allow to happen. It came out at one of their weekly meetings that they had all been made to sign a pre-nuptial before marrying their present husbands. The only way they would get nothing is if their husbands divorced them.

They knew a plan must be formed to cut off any likelihood of that ever happening to any of them. Now the weekly luncheons turned from a friendly get together to a weekly planning meeting. It took weeks to get all the details put into place. Once that was done they agreed to carry out the mission.

Lauren smiled, inside she was congratulating herself on what has been accomplished so far. Soon all the women would have exactly what they want. Somewhere deep down buried in a dark corner of her soul she felt a twinge of regret for the way they had achieved what was rightfully theirs. But the rewards far outweighed that tiny spot of conscience. She brushed it aside as she ran her pearl handled brush over her sable brown hair. None of them would go back to tending bars or waiting tables ever again.

This is their lives now and it will stay that way.

Clark had finished his job of searching the names of the friends of the Wesley's by closing time. He printed out the sheets and handed them to Stella before leaving the office for the day.

Stella's trip out to see Betty got her no further. Although she knew she was inside, she still refused to answer the door. This time Stella wrote a small note and shoved it in the crack of the door hoping that would get Betty to call her. Then she returned to her office to do some searching of her own.

Stella did a quick glance at the papers before packing them in her bag and headed out for home. She knew she would beat George there by an hour or so.

When she got home, Graves opened the door for her. It still made her itch to have servants in the house. He welcomed her home and took her jacket. She didn't miss the way he looked down his nose at her. Although he was always cordial to her, she felt the chill from him and couldn't figure out what he has against her. She knew it was the cook's night off and that lifted her spirits a bit and made her do a little happy dance in her head. She couldn't wait to take off her shoulder holster, as she dashed towards the kitchen.

Graves must have alerted the kitchen staff to clear out seeing where the Mistress was heading since there was no one in the large kitchen when she entered it.

Once inside the huge industrial sized kitchen she wiggled her hips in anticipation of using the stainless steel equipment. Stella decided on fixing the salad first and rifled through the large refrigerator for all the ingredients she needed.

God it was a chef's dream inside the huge chrome unit. She began to pull out fresh vegetables she knew were picked from the garden out back and washed and laid them on the huge cutting board. Selecting the right knife from the block she chopped each one in turn and placed them in a large bowl. Then mixing up a salad dressing, she placed it and the bowl of salad back inside the fridge to keep them good while she got busy with the main course.

Stella pulled out two large pork chops, some mushrooms, an onion and cheese. The mushrooms and onions she placed in a pan with olive oil and butter and began to sauté them slowly. As they were cooking she dug out some fingerling potatoes, washed them, seasoned them and placed them in the oven to bake. By that time the mushrooms were ready. Taking the chops, she sliced them and stuffed them with the mushroom and onions and grated cheese and seasoned the chops before placing them in the oven.

George found her in the kitchen and watched her prepare supper. She looked so relaxed and happy. Watching her, it occurred to him that this was something she missed doing. Seeing the delight on her face he wondered if he could talk the cook into taking an extra night or two off each month.

She sensed him and turned around closing the oven door. It was crazy she knew, but just having him standing there looking at her the way he did had heat flare up in her center. She caught herself wiping her mouth with the back of her hand from the saliva suddenly pooling in her mouth that the look in his eyes caused. All thoughts of pre-dinner appetizers flew away as the heat spread turning her bones to jelly where she stood.

George saw her eyes glaze over and watched her body loosening up. The blood rushed down from his head pounding in his loins. The need was building so fast he practically flew the length of the kitchen to touch her, to feel her, to taste her. His breath caught in his lungs and released the moment his mouth was on hers. The sweet taste, her taste had him begging for more. His clothes strained as his pulsing need grew and grew, aching for release. He had to have his hands on her.

Stella tasted his mouth sending her needs soaring. She had to feel his skin on hers. She tore at his clothes as he did hers. Then as they wrapped themselves around each other naked they floated up. Sparks shot out from them as flames licked through them from the inside. With one hard thrust he was buried deep inside her in a hot moist vice. They both swallowed each other's deep, all consuming passion filled groans.

George held still for a moment so as not give in to the need to empty there and then. It took all that he was to not give in to that need and begin a slow in and out, in and out hard pulsating thumping motion. He felt her build, build until he knew she was reaching the crest. With one final hard thrust he emptied, throwing them both over. She quivered in his embrace on the slow descent down to the cool tiled floor.

They were in the kitchen, or rather on the kitchen floor. The water was here and magic was allowed. Stella knew she had only to wait for it. Sweaty and sated she concentrated on gathering oxygen into her air starved lungs. She did not even have the strength to sit up.

Through the ringing in her ears she heard him whisper a chant and two large frosted glasses of water sat next to them on the floor. It took all her strength to lift one and sip from it. She finished the last of hers in one large gulp.

Now that her thirst was quenched she sat next to him on the floor and took inventory. The kitchen was strewn with their clothes and they were a mess. A shower was first in order and then she would finish preparing supper. God they now succeeded in christening three rooms of the house. That thought had her smile widen.

Supper had to wait just a bit longer as they both enjoyed a round of shower sex. Once dried off and dressed they both went down limber and sated, in the lust area at least. Stella's stomach rumbled on the way downstairs.

She shooed him out of the kitchen before he had other ideas in order to finish cooking the meal for them. It seemed they were never truly fully sated in their lust for each other. And that was a very good thing in her mind.

Sitting at the table over the first course, Stella felt guilty about keeping the information she found to herself. She knew her part in the investigation closed when she returned Binky to his owners, but damn it she knew these strings of murders were involved somehow even if the Mayor's family were hit by copycats.

George sat quietly eating watching her play with her food. Something was up and he had the feeling she was trying to keep something from him. He did not like that part of it. He could not tolerate secrets in their relationship. He decided to give it until the meal was over and if she did not tell him what was on her mind, he would drag it out of her, one way or another.

George marveled at her culinary skills. The food was delicious. If she hadn't chosen the profession she had, she could have made a top notch chef. When the meal was over, Stella brought the coffee in on a trolley to the library. Graves usually performed this act, but she didn't want him around her tonight. She did get some rather strange looks from the kitchen staff however, when she requested they make up the trolley for her.

George watched her pour it before settling herself down beside him on the sofa. It was time to do some digging.

"You were very quiet at dinner Stella. Did you have a difficult day?" He wound his finger around strands of her flaming hair. She had left it loose and flowing after her shower.

"What?" lost in her own thoughts, his voice brought her back. "Oh, no, it was a pretty productive day. How about you?" She side stepped his question.

"We haven't gotten any further with the investigation. We are missing something, I'm sure of it." He frowned showing his frustration.

"Why don't you tell me about your day?" He felt her stiffen slightly.

Stella took a sip of her coffee trying to bide time. She didn't feel comfortable keeping secrets from him. But if she told him her theory he would want to take over. It was foolish to feel this way, she knew, and they were married. They were a unit and had worked together more times than she liked. No, if this was going to make her feel this way, she had no other option but to tell him. Doing otherwise would put a wall between them and she didn't think she could bear that. She put her cup down on the table and turned to him.

"Okay, I think I know the connection you and the squad are missing." She started off slowly.

"And you were going to sit on that? You were planning on keeping what you know from me? Tell me why Stella?"

She looked into his eyes and saw the hurt in them. Her heart nearly broke and she knew then that she was wrong to try to keep it from him for her own selfishness. Maybe it had something to do with not wanting to give up any of her independence, she didn't know. But she did know now that it was the wrong decision.

"I don't know why I didn't tell you earlier. Maybe I just wanted to be able to work a case on my own without anyone's help. But I can see I was wrong to do that. I'm sorry George." She reached up cupped his face and pressed her lips gently to his.

He saw it in her eyes. The war she had been battling with herself and it eased some of the anger he had felt towards her.

"We are a unit Stella. What affects one affects the other. You are still and always will be a very strong woman. A woman who knows how to and can do her job, and do it very well. We will always have cases that connect. That does not mean either one of us will try to take over. We will work together; we are not in a contest my darling." George stroked the side of her face with his fingers.

What he forgot is the way he has been forcing himself in on her cases when they connect with the Police. At those times he never realized how that makes her feel; only that he feels justified in stepping in taking charge like any cop would.

"I know, I guess it will just take me time to learn how to share." She gave him a smile.

"Good, now are you willing to tell me about this connection you found?"

Stella took a deep breath and told him everything she had found out so far. When she finished she found her spirits rise up and the load she didn't know she carried lifted.

Stella told him her suspicions of the murders being done by inside help. She gave him the rundown on some of the wives on the list Clark came up with. Although she hadn't worked out the reason behind the murders, she felt that the group of women, meeting on a weekly basis, is somehow involved in some way. It was only a theory of hers' that it had to do with keeping a certain lifestyle.

SEVEN

Geoorge went into work the next day feeling lighter. What Stella laid out to him had him agreeing to the possibility of it. A bunch of social climbers bent on keeping the lifestyles they had grown accustomed to does have a lot of merit and made sense of the lack of evidence.

It made even more sense knowing the men, coming from wealthy families, who married these women more than likely had them all sign a pre-nuptial contract. And if in fact this is the case, all those women would be left without a penny should the men decide to end the marriages.

George was a bit angry with himself and his squad. Just because the wives had a solid alibi didn't mean they shouldn't have checked into their lives. They may have come up with the same theory as Stella had they done this.

Stella was sitting in her office leaning back in her chair staring at her crime board. She had put all the information on it she got from Bentley and the searches done by Clark. In her mind she could see the pattern. It was a very clever plan and it was going to be very hard to prove. Now that she told George what she knew, she had to let the police take it from there.

She knew the women weren't done and there was no telling who was going to be the next victim until they found out which wife was planning a little vacation for herself. She knew George would put a detail on the remaining women and find the next victim hopefully in time to save his life. Her case for the Mayor's son is closed but her new case is with her new client Bentley.

She shrugged her shoulders. She checked her watch and found it was nearly time to head over to her one o'clock meeting with Percival Beecham.

Stella pulled up in front of the Belvedere, parked, got out and went into the lobby. She did not bother with the desk but headed straight to the elevator and pushed the button for his floor. He was waiting for her opening the door on her first knock.

Coffee was set up in the spacious living area. Percival had placed all his papers on the long glass table in front of the blue leaf print sofa. Stella settled down on the sofa taking her cup and glancing at the volume of paperwork he had documented on this case. She noticed he had separated them into piles representing the countries involved in the thefts. 'Very organized,' she thought.

"Okay, take me through what you have here." She set her cup down and took out her own notebook.

Percival lost no time going through them slowly and meticulously one by one, starting with the first theft. She wrote in her own version of shorthand all the pertinent facts. One by one they went through each case. By the time they finished, they had gone through two pots of coffee.

Stella sat back running the information in her head. He was not only organized but very thorough. And he was right about one thing, the thief or thieves were very good. They left no part of themselves at any of the crime scenes. Someone in that group was very knowledgeable about forensics or had some help in that area.

The one thing that piqued her interest was the fact that there was no sign of a break in. That hit too close to the case George was working on. When you have eliminated all other means, you were left with the obvious. They had inside help on all the jewel thefts, either from Lloyds of London, or the victims' homes.

"Does Lloyds of London have a branch of home security installations?" She asked him.

"Yes we do security as well as insurance." Percival was shocked that he had not thought to link that to his cases.

"Were the insurance policies on all the jewels stolen put through by one agent or different agents of Lloyds of London?" Her mind was fitting pieces of the puzzle together.

His eyebrows winged up as he caught the meaning behind her question. It had never occurred to him to look at the company for this. Lloyds of London has always been the most highly respected company in the world. All its' agents were thoroughly vetted, bonded and known for being the best for their honesty and discretion. Never would he ever consider that someone in the company could betray it. But now that this woman mentioned the possibility, he could not in good conscience dismiss the idea.

Percival reached over and went through each file to find the agent's name on the insurance policy to check for himself. Angry with himself for missing such obvious clues, he frowned up at her.

"It appears that all but one was written up by a David Montgomery. The third case was written by a Peter Combe." Seeing it in black and white, it stung him deep that an agent of such a prestigious company could even contemplate being a party of this.

Stella watched him take it in. She felt sorry for him. It was probably in his nature or maybe just the British culture he grew up in that gave him airs and made him act like a snob so she really couldn't hold that against him. This was cutting him deep which made her bend a bit to feel sympathy for him. But sorry or not, he had to wake up to the facts.

"You would have more access to the records in your company than I would. If you want to dig into the background of the two agents, I'll take the names of the homes that were hit and the names of the insured here in this area." She suggested. "Why don't you give me the list and call me when your search is completed." Stella opened her notebook to a new page to enter the names and address. Once she had them written down she got up.

"One more thing before I go, why did you come all the way here when you could have called me from England?" She stood by the door looking back at him.

"You could say I was playing a hunch. Tracking the locations of the hits, I have a strong feeling that your country was next on the list. We presently hold the insurance policy on some very high quality jewels in this area. I believe the city is called Paris Ontario. The family is the Sheldon's."

"And who is the agent on that policy?" She had a hunch too and hers were usually right.

"David Montgomery," he said softly.

"Well then, I think with what we just learned a phone call to that family may be in order. I'll leave that to you as well. After you contact them, call me and fill me in and we will go from there." Stella turned and walked out leaving him standing in the doorway with a dejected look. She knew her conversation with him had hit a few nerves, but he was British after all and would soon bounce back. Stiff upper lip and all that, she smiled to herself.

When she got back to her office, she was surprised to find Louise waiting for her in one of the chairs sipping coffee and carrying on a lively conversation with Clark. She noticed Clark's face was beet red almost hiding his adorable freckles.

"Some of us work for a living Louise," Stella greeted them on her way over to her desk. "Did you come here to flirt with my assistant or did you want to see me for something?"

"Oh I came to see you and found this adorable young man sitting here working like a slave," she cooed at Clark batting her eyelashes making him blush even deeper.

"Down Louise, you do remember Dave don't you?" she lifted an eyebrow at her. "Clark I will have some names for you to check as soon I receive the list." She swallowed the laugh looking at his beet red face. She just shook her head knowing he was out of his league with someone like Louise.

"Okay Louise, what did you want to see me about?" She turned her attention on the blonde sitting across from her.

Louise swiveled around in her chair to face Stella, a smile still on her face from the reaction she brought out in Clark. "I just wanted to let you know that the Belvedere is booked for the shower and Angela is on board for the decorations. The shower is planned for three weeks from this weekend."

"You could have called me to tell me all this Louise." Stella frowned. "You didn't have to come all the way over here and spend time flirting with Clark to tell me."

"Oh, but look at all the fun I would have missed if I did things your way Stella." Louise grinned.

"Uh, huh," was all Stella said, pinning her with a look.

"Okay, okay, I could have called." Louise relented. "Look, you make it perfectly clear that your schedule does not permit you to join in on the meetings for the event. I thought I would come over and bring you up to date and get any input you care to offer. This is your best friend's wedding shower after all."

Oh that hit the mark, Stella now felt full of guilt at having others do the planning while she ran around working her cases. She knew she was letting Deb down putting all the arrangements onto the others. She cleared her mind and decided to give Louise her full attention.

"Okay, I'm all ears. Tell me what has been planned out so far and what you need from me. Knowing Deb, the event will have to be way over the top, and knowing you, you have a theme all picked out. That's what all you women do isn't it? Make a theme for every event?"

"Well that's just it Stella, the theme is stumping us all. The rest of the planning, your family and I can do. We just cannot agree on a theme. I was hoping maybe you had an idea for that."

"So what have you all come up with so far?" This was one area she was clueless in.

"We were desperate so don't laugh," Louise pouted. "Deb is like this energizer bunny half the time so we thought of rabbits. Angela laughed and pooh-poohed that one. Then Gwen thought about pixies because Deb looks like one. But that was kind of the same theme she put on for you. So you see we really can't come up with anything we can all agree on."

A light bulb went on in Stella's head. "Have you thought about what she is? Deb is the top fashion designer. Why not make the theme look like a fashion show and Angela can do most of the arranging for that?

After all that's what she does for a living and she knows Deb's taste."

"Oh God, Stella, you are brilliant. Yes, yes that will be absolutely perfect. I just know the rest will go along with that." Louise clapped her hands together. "There, that will be your contribution and I know Deb will be thrilled to tears. I can just see it now. God you're a genius Stella."

"If only my cases were this easy to solve Louise. Glad I could help." Stella couldn't help grinning as she watched Louise actually bounce in her chair while still clapping her hands in joy.

All the while Louise was in the office, poor Clark could not diminish the red blush on his face. It was embarrassing. Just hearing Louise's sexy voice kept it blooming no matter how hard he tried not to hear it. Her perfume lingered in his nostrils even after she had gone. His heart raced inside his chest. It was his first real crush.

Stella was too busy to notice her assistant's obvious discomfort. She began a crime board and taking out her notebook she logged everything on it in chronological order. When she was done, she stood back and examined what was there.

"Not just thieves, but international thieves." She muttered to herself. "And according to the timetable they were hitting twice a month. It would probably take a week or two to fence the take." She did not figure they had a regular job and they could afford to fly from country to country. She turned at the sound of her fax machine.

Stella walked over and waited for the machine to finish spitting out the sheets of paper. It was a lengthy list of names. She gave Clark the paper with the names of the homes already hit and she took the one with the possible homes with her to her desk. This was going to take some time to do the searches on all of them.

Since Percival felt the home in Paris was the next target, she started with that one. She pulled up her search program and keyed in the names of Mr. and Mrs. Leonard Sheldon. He was the owner and CEO of Winegard Industries after buying it out over ten years ago. They manufacture software and are a blue chip company in the stock market.

She checked both Leonard and his wife Celeste and found they were both wealthy in their own right. No criminal records on either one. They produced two children, one of each and they also have no run-ins with the law. They contribute to charities and Celeste chairs on a few charity organizations. All in all a normal family, she thought, other than the fact of them being rich. Checking further, she noticed that they bought their security system from Lloyds of London.

Tingle.

Well Percival had every right to think they would be on the list of the thieves. It was just going to be a matter of figuring out the thieves' time table for the hit.

It was time to call in the reserves. Dave Palmer was the best security guy she knew. Stella called him and filled him in on the case. After telling him she was strongly in favour of Percival guessing that the Sheldon's were being the target for the thieves, she asked him to put a couple of men on their home to stake it out.

Dave was always glad to help Stella out. Ever since she went into the Private Investigator field, they had worked a lot of cases together. Her doing the investigation and him supplying the security. Now that he was engaged to George's foster sister, he considered himself part of the family. One thing about Stella, life and work was never boring.

After she hung up the phone, Stella sat back in her chair and looked over at Clark, who was busy running searches and writing down his findings. Her gut told her he would come up empty. The list he was working on wasn't going to point to the victims for this, but it was good practice for him. She decided to call Percival and tell him about the security she arranged for the Sheldon's.

As she reached for the phone it rang.

"Blake Private Investigator," she answered.

"Miss Blake," she heard Percival's thick accent. "I thought I would ring you and tell you I found something. Had you not pointed me in the direction you did, I believe I would have overlooked the obvious." He was miffed with himself that he hadn't thought to look within his own company.

"You found a connection with the agent and the security department?"

"I believe I have Miss Blake. It appears that David Montgomery and a certain employee in the security department have been doing a little business on the side so to speak."

"Well, some people do like to take on extra work. It seems that Lloyds of London will be in the market to hire more personnel in the near future." She grinned.

"With the information I unearthed and forwarded to the head of the company, I would say hiring will begin very soon but with a bit more care to the background checks."

"Alerting them now may result in alerting the thieves. But of course you probably thought of that."

Once again she was a step ahead of him and it was not going down well. Now he had to call his office and stop them from dismissing the two men.

"Yes, well I felt I should call you with my results Miss Blake."

"Before you hang up I thought I would let you know that I have put a detail on the Sheldon's home. Should they be the next target, we will be able to stop the thieves before they can make off with anything."

"Thank you for your assistance in this matter Miss Blake. Of course you will receive your percentage once this is closed."

Stella heard the phone click in her ear. "Oh, I think I just made his day." She laughed.

Clark looked over at her at the sound of her laughter. She really gets a kick out her work, he thought. Here was a case that started outside the country and with very little if any evidence or clues to go on and she nails it in less than two days.

What Clark didn't know is that this Percival guy had all the information but didn't put it together right. Had he done that he might not have needed to look for outside help? It is the way Stella arranges data to get results is what he's come to her to learn.

Clark envied her brain and instincts, the way she looks at things and pieces them together even with the missing pieces. That was the reason he applied for the position of her assistant, to find out how she does it and how to copy it. He would be the top journalist on the globe with a brain like hers.

"Do you still want me to continue with the searches? It sounds like you have this case pretty much wrapped up." His eyes were wide with amazement.

"It's never a good idea to leave anything undone. You never know when situations turn around to try and take a bite out of you. Always have all your bases covered and all the information gathered. Who knows, you might come up with something that could lead to a different answer."

'And that's why she is the best,' he thought again. This is a very valuable lesson for him.

Since Stella felt she had done everything she could for Percival, she decided to try one more time to talk to Betty Vanhorn. She got up picked up her bag and without saying a word headed out.

Now Clark frowned at this.

Damn it all to Hell and back. She keeps taking off without letting him know where she's going and why. It's like she suddenly forgets I'm even here and simply ignores me. She just pretty much solved this international case and now without a word or glance she's off to who knows where? 'How can I learn if she isn't willing to take the time to fill me in? How am I supposed to figure out what is going on in her head?' Clark growled. 'Stella knows this is the reason I've come to her, to learn from her. But if she's not willing to teach me then I'm just wasting my time.'

EIGHT

Stella walked up to Betty's door and knocked. This time she decided to keep knocking until Betty opens the door. The constant persisting knocking finally had Betty relenting and the door opening just a crack to peek one eye out.

"Please go away. I don't want to talk to you. I . . . I'm not well." Betty spoke through the crack in the door.

Stella was having none of it. She pushed hard on the door sending Betty back a couple of steps. She walked in and closed the door behind her.

"Mrs. Vanhorn," Stella towered over the plump older woman. "I am very sorry for barging in like this but we need to talk." She pinned her with a look.

Stella noticed how pale her skin was and the way she kept wringing her hands together. Her nerves have definitely taken their toll on this poor woman. Stella doubted that this woman had eaten anything in the last two days. Her eyes were all puffy as if she had been on a crying jag.

Stella gently laid her hand on her round shoulder and steered her into one of the rooms off the hallway. She pushed her down into a worn recliner and sat on the table set before it to look straight at her.

"Mrs. Vanhorn," Stella started off softly. "I know you are scared. Bentley is very worried about you. He told your employers that you are ill and taking a few days off." She let that soak in before continuing and noticed a flash of relief on Betty's face that her employers did not know the truth.

"I . . . I am ill," she stuttered. "Please don't kill me," she almost passed out.

"No, you are not ill, what you are, is scared. You are scared right down to the bone and I think I know the reason for it. And I'm not here to kill you but to help you."

Any colour that was in her face now drained away. Stella was worried she might pass out on her at any moment. She looked around for something to give her. Since there was no bar in the room, she didn't want to leave her alone, she reached over took her hand and gently patted it.

"Betty, may I call you Betty?" she got a nod from the woman before continuing. "Betty, I believe you overheard a conversation in the Wesley home which has you terrified." She gripped her hand when it jerked, to keep contact with her. "I believe you overheard Mrs. Wesley discussing certain plans, plans that involve her friends and murder."

Betty let out a scream, she swayed, her eyes rolled back in her head and she fainted. Now Stella did leave her to look for something to give her to drink and a cold cloth for her head. All she could find was a bottle of juice in the fridge so she poured a glass and wet a dishcloth that was lying on the counter and went back in to revive the terrified woman. Some women just couldn't handle the seedier side of life, she thought.

Oh well. At any other time she abhorred this weak trait but her heart did go out to this poor woman.

When she brought her around, Betty looked around at her surroundings and then her eyes filled with fear and then filled with tears that spilled down her plump cheeks onto her round bosoms.

She buried her face in her hands and wept. "Oh Miss, oh Miss, I'm so scared. If the Mistress finds out that I heard her talking to Miss Brianna and what they were saying I know they will kill me. I can't go back there, I'm so scared. I thought she sent you here to kill me."

And there it was, Stella thought. Now she just had to pry it out of her. She took out her recorder and laid it on the table in front of them. "Betty, no one knows you overheard anything. I was not sent by the Mistress. Bentley doesn't even know the real reason you left. He is protecting you like a good friend does. Now tell me what you heard. Take your time and tell me. I promise I will not let anything happen to you."

It was all too much. Knowing what she knows and keeping it to herself, living scared from one moment to another was just too much. She looked up into those long sea-green eyes and saw the determination in them and also seeing that this woman was telling her the truth.

She had to trust someone. Seeing Stella' gun peeking out and not using it on her helped to gain some trust. But if she has to die she prayed it will be quick and painless.

The fear she had been living with was enough on its own to kill her. Betty took a deep breath then straightened up in the chair and prepared herself to take a leap of faith or to face her death.

"You look so strong for someone so young and I just can't go on living this way. I don't know if I can believe you when you say you won't harm me and can protect me. But I just can't live this way." She took another deep breath before continuing.

"The last day I worked, Miss Brianna stopped over to visit the Mistress. Bentley had me prepare a tea tray for them, which I did. After that I got busy with my work and later Bentley brought the tray back in. But I noticed that it was missing a spoon. I didn't want to bother Bentley, so I thought I would just slip out and collect it myself. You see, I thought Miss Brianna had already left." She paused to wipe her damp palms on her skirt.

"I was just on the other side of the door to the lounge and about to enter when I heard them laughing. I would have turned around and gone back to the kitchen but the Mistress mentioned the name of their other friend's late husband and I heard them both giggle. Well that did not sound right to me. I would never have thought the Mistress to be cruel like that. I have to say I was so upset over that, that I stayed where I was and did the most unpardonable thing. I eavesdropped on the Mistress."

Stella could see that caused her a lot of distress, and waited for her to tell her the rest of it.

"Miss Brianna said she couldn't believe how easy it was and surprised that they all got away with it. Then the Mistress said to her that the plan was perfect and that soon they would all be able to have the lives they were meant to have and no one would be able to take it away from them. She said all they had to do was to keep to the plan and they would all be free of any threat of divorce from their husbands. They would be free women to live as they choose."

"Miss I think they murdered those two men, the ones married to the Mistress' friends." Her eyes had gone wide and Stella feared she was going to faint again.

Stella started patting the back of her hand again to keep her from collapsing. "I think they are all in on the murders too Betty and you were right to leave the house. Your Mistress does not know that you overheard her conversation with her friend, but I think it safer for you to stay away until the police can do their job and arrest them. If you would like, I can have a bodyguard brought here to stay with you until this is over."

"Oh Miss, yes please. I have been so scared. Can he be big and strong? Maybe if he was a big strong man, I might feel a little safer."

"Sure, I'll get you one of the biggest and strongest bodyguards Dave has to offer," she smiled at the little plump woman. "I want you to stay here. If you need anything, you just tell your bodyguard and he'll arrange to have it brought here. Okay?"

"Oh thank you Miss. Can you please tell Bentley thank you for me? And tell him that I will be safe now. He is such a dear, dear man and a very good friend."

"I'll tell Bentley. The police will want a statement from you. If it makes you feel more comfortable I can arrange to have them come here to get it."

Betty nervously agreed.

Stella got up and put through the call to David's office. Once that was arranged and the bodyguard showed up, Stella left Betty with her big strong man. She shook her head on the way to her car. She never could understand how some women thought muscles on a man were enough to chase away their fears.

She headed back to her office to collect the paperwork Clark had done and locking up before heading home. She managed to beat George by five minutes. The cook was working today so puttering in the kitchen was out of the question. She handed Graves her jacket and went upstairs to take a shower.

Stella had just finished washing her hair and was in the process of lathering body wash all over her when a familiar pair of hands reached around and cupped her breasts bringing out a moan and instant heat. She reached behind her and grabbed hold of a pair of strong muscular butt cheeks reminding her how completely toned his body is. Then feeling her way on the hard body behind her, found him. She wrapped her hand around him, finding him hard and ready she heard him suck in his breath as she firmed up her grip on him. Smiling she turned sought his mouth. They both dove in taking the kiss deeper, drinking in each other's taste like thirsty travelers.

George's hands travelled down to cup her and swallowed her groan of ecstasy. He spread her and with one long hard thrust he entered her and held. They both shivered with need. The hot steamy water felt cold compared to the heat building and pouring out of them. The shower filled with steam and sparks from their building passions. She matched him thrust for thrust, in and out, in and out. Their wet bodies slapping against each other brought them both closer to fulfillment. When he felt her tighten around him he knew she was reaching the peak. He climbed with her and with one final deep hard thrust he sent them both over the edge.

Legs limp and unsteady, she clung hard to him in order to stay upright. Her whole body felt like jelly and it felt wonderful. They stayed twined together until they felt they could stand on their own. George rained kisses over her face and held her tight against him just to keep her close for another minute.

Heaven could not be better than this, he thought.

When he felt her strain away, he loosened his grip knowing the moment had passed. Reluctantly he let her step back and allow once again for life to continue. They finished showering and stepped out of the shower to towel off.

Now that they were showered and hormonally sated, sort of, they sat in the dining room enjoying the delicious meal and their usual shop-talk conversation.

"I'll send one of the detectives over to Mrs. Vanhorn's tomorrow. With her statement and what you found out it shouldn't be long before we have this case wrapped up." He glanced over at her noting that she was picking at her food.

"Stella, I know you wanted to be the one to close the case, but it has to be done by the police. I want you to know that this case wouldn't be closing if it wasn't for all the work you did. You are the one that solved it sweetheart."

"George you don't have to placate me. I know it was my work that solved it and I also know that I had to turn it over to you. I'm just being selfish and greedy. If I was still on the force it would be me that interviews those murdering bunch of women. And believe me, I'd get them all to spill their guts, but on the other hand I really like being a Private Investigator. It seems I'm a little torn between the two. I'll get over it, don't worry."

"Would watching from the observation room help?" he suggested knowing she would want to see it through.

"Thanks, yeah I'd like that. I want to see their faces when they realize their perfect plan had flaws and it's those flaws that will put them behind bars. God George, they murdered their husbands just so they can keep up the pretense of being high society. It makes me sick." She stabbed at her lobster salad.

What she didn't want to say is how she felt George and the squad let her down by not coming up with the answers she did. They had every opportunity to dig into the wives' lives and yet they let that slip. She only followed all the facts that they had and should have dug into the way she did.

"Thank goodness you are filthy rich in your own right," he laughed making her laugh too.

"So how is the international case coming along?" George switched the conversation to take her mind off the case.

"Lloyds of London will be doing some hiring. It seems they have a couple of employees in their employ that have some very criminal minded side jobs. If Percival Beecham is right, there should be a couple of very surprised thieves out of work as well." That brightened her spirits enough to have her do justice to the meal in front of her.

Seeing the light back in her eyes made George feel better about taking the other case from her.

"Well I'd say you have had a very productive day Miss Stella Blake Private Investigator." He grinned at her.

Stella's eyes brightened even more as a thought raced through her head. "Yeah, it's been a busy week and the best part of it is that no ghosts have popped up the whole time. All in all I'd say it was a great week."

"Oh, I almost forgot," George couldn't hide the mischievous glint in his eyes. "Louise called me to tell me how much you helped her with her plans for the wedding shower. A fashion theme, now that was brilliant Stella."

"Yeah, yeah, I have my moments." Then she frowned. "I really should be doing more for Deb. She is my best friend. I feel like a heel not putting more time in on the shower arrangements."

"Stella, Deb is your best friend and she knows how busy you are. The work you do takes up most of your time. I'm sure she understands that. And now that both your cases are all but done, you will have time to give some attention to the shower plans."

"She's my only real friend and yes you're right, I can put in the effort to see that she has the best wedding shower ever. She deserves it and I want to make her happy." Stella determined.

The rest of the meal was eaten in a quiet harmony. They took their coffee into the library to relax.

Lauren Wesley was relaxing in a different way. Bertrum retired early as was his habit. She had the whole evening to herself to go over the schedule Celine gave her on her husband. Celine would be leaving for her little private vacation leaving her husband home for a few days without her.

Celine had noticed recently the difference in her husband's affections towards her and feared the worst. She was sure he was seeing someone else and it would only be a matter of time before he wanted a divorce. She could not bear to go back to having nothing after living the life of the rich.

Lauren had the spare keys Celine had made for her and the codes to the alarm system. Now she studied Johnathan Foxworth's personal private schedule and habits. After tomorrow night Celine will never have to fear losing everything she worked so hard to obtain. Another happy thought was that after tomorrow night, she wanted to be next on the list she and her friends had made a pact about.

God, she couldn't wait to get rid of Bertrum. He was boring and one thing about Lauren was that she hated boredom most of all. Another thing she found out about herself was that she had a real talent for planning murder and out-witting the police. She smiled to herself wondering where this newly found talent would take her next.

Lauren sat at her vanity in her dressing room, preening herself. In the mirror she saw a wealthy high-class woman staring back at her. In her mind the vision looking back at her was nothing more than her true right to be. This is what she should have been born into instead of from those low-class parents of hers. 'God how could they stand to live that life all these years,' she thought. If only her parents had a modicum of ambition, they could have made a better life for themselves. They should have put more effort into finding a way to climb the ladder to success and made themselves wealthy instead of just eking out a moderate income. It was beyond her to find some people happy to wallow in mediocre.

NINE

George sat in his office going over everything Stella told him with his squad of detectives. He ordered a stake-out on the list of women whose husbands were still alive and well. He saw the questioning look in his squad's eyes as to how their old LT. came by the information, but they were wise enough not to give way to vocalizing their curiosity.

George never gave it a thought as to the way Stella found out this information and what led her to it. Once they discovered the wives had a solid alibi they never questioned it. This is one mistake he will discover later and will learn from it and so will his squad.

It always fascinated them as to how she was able to come up with the solutions when there was next to no evidence to back it up. This new LT. was good and they accepted him but to them he would never be the LT. Stella was.

"That's quite a scheme this group of women have concocted, if it's true." Sally spoke up. "But we still have one big problem; LT. there is no evidence of any kind to back up this theory, all the wives have alibis."

"I'm glad you brought that up Sally. It so happens that we also have a witness that overheard a conversation pointing the crimes to these women, and a recorded statement."

"Where is the witness?" Tom leaned forward in his chair.

"For now the witness is under protection, but we got a written statement outlining what was overheard."

"Why hasn't this witness been brought in so we can question this person?" Tom demanded.

"Look, I know this is not procedure, but it was the only way we could get a statement. The witness is too scared to be seen in the open. If it makes you feel any better, this witness talked to Stella and agreed to give a statement as long as it could be done at where the witness is staying." George leaned back in his chair. "I'm willing to accept the terms and hope that you will go along with them as well. This is the first real break we've had in this case."

Mentioning Stella's name had them ease back and each one nodded their heads in agreement. They trusted her judgment implicitly.

George noticed how they were willing to give Stella blind trust where he was still trying to gain that trust from them. He knew right then that he had a very large pair of shoes to fill for this team to accept him the way they do her.

To hear them accept without question or hesitation what she brought to the table showed him he has a lot of work ahead of him to gain even a modicum of that kind of trust from them. Hearing their reaction to her findings told him that they all held her in very high esteem. This gave him more insight into how she ran this squad before he took it over. According to the entire precinct, Stella was the best of the best while she worked here.

'God, how was anyone supposed to fill those shoes?' he thought. 'And how was anyone to lead a squad if they are not respected or trusted?' George knew in that moment that he has to come up with a way for his squad to look at him and trust and respect him the way they do for her.

All the time he spent on the Force in another city he never ran into this kind of problem before. He held the respect of everyone he worked with back then. He was never questioned about the way he worked before even though he did everything in the Human way.

George did know that Stella was in denial of her bloodline while she worked on this Force. Her superior record and the way she dealt with all members on this Force had them all willing to follow and work with her. It was more in the way she looked at the law and followed all the rules in the rulebook that had everyone holding her in the highest of respect. Once she made Lieutenant, she treated all those under her with fairness even when she had to mete out discipline. It is a tall order for anyone stepping into her position. George just hopes that in time he can gain the squads' total acceptance and trust. He does know that she will not be coming back to take over the squad again.

While George was holding his meeting, Celine was busy packing her bags. The limo would be arriving soon to take her to the airport. She had given the servants all their instructions for the next few days that she would be away and now she concentrated on packing her things and daydreaming of a life she worked hard to achieve.

When the limo arrived she was ready. The chauffer put her luggage into the trunk and helped her in before taking his place behind the wheel. He drove down the long driveway and through the open gates turning toward the way that would take them to the airport. The gates closed behind them.

The stake-out arrived to park far enough away to still be able to watch the gates guarding the estate minutes after the limo had driven out of sight. They just missed their chance.

Stella sat behind her desk going through the files. There was nothing more she could do for Percival or Bentley. She had called the Paris Police Department to give them her information and a heads-up. She let them know that she had people watching the house and they should contact them.

She'd done all she could with Dave's men watching the home of the next target of the international thieves and George was in control of catching the women before the next murder could be committed. Time, she thought, to pull out another case and get down to doing her own work.

She had a half a dozen files on her desk and was going through them one by one when a large oval ring appeared before her. The edges shot out diamond sparkled lights and Ravena's face appeared inside it. Her brilliant red hair adorned by a jewel encrusted crown, her green eyes filled with worry looked down at Stella.

Stella rose and bowed her head. "My Queen," she said.

"Stella, my dear daughter, I am so sorry to come to you with trouble."

"What is it mother?" suddenly Stella's heart skipped a beat. Queen Ravena never came to her without her calling for her first. Something must be terribly wrong. "Has something happened to Prince Gareg or Prince Gavin?" For only worry about those two would cause her Queen to seek her out.

"They are well Stella, but we do have a serious problem and we need your help."

"Anything my Queen." Stella bowed deeper.

"I am so sorry to bring you this news. It appears that Gobrath is seeking a way to open a portal to bring his father into my world. We have searched high and low for him and cannot find him. It was only through a disenchanted muse that we found out about his plans. Sabrina had fallen for his charms and when he cast her off for another she came to me asking for forgiveness and told me of his plan."

"Mother, if the King of the Warlock world enters yours none of you are safe and he could find a way to enter mine bringing Gobrath with him. All worlds as we know them will be destroyed."

"That is why I have called you my dear. I'm afraid it will take the combined power of your father, you, and Gavin to fight this."

Stella could see true fear in her Queen's eyes. She feared for her world but most of all she feared for her son.

"Tell me what I have to do and I promise it will be done." She vowed.

"Oh my daughter I can never thank you enough for your undying loyalty. We will keep on searching for Gobrath. Once we find him I will call upon you again. With you and your father and me, Gareg and Gavin, we will combine our powers to face him. Gareg and I will be working day and night on a spell that we hope will erase from his memory of how to open a portal. Once we find him and the three of you bind him, we can cast the spell. But first we have to find the spell. I pray we can find it in time."

"My Queen you only have to ask and it will be done. I'll tell Garrett right away and have him ready for the moment you need us."

"Thank you my daughter. And again I am so sorry that I had to bring trouble to your door once again."

"I am always here to serve you my Queen. We will be ready for you."

Ravena paused and looked at Stella. "I notice that you do not call the one that sired you Father," Ravena frowned.

"My Queen, in my World Warlocks mate with Elfin blood and then leave them once the Elfin blood conceives. This has never given them the status for that title. Garrett only returned to my mother once I was fully grown. I do not think of him of being anything other than another Warlock, but with special gifts. I've never missed him. My work brought me close to another person that I have grown to think of as a father and I'm quite content with that." She told her.

"I see," Ravena frowned. This told her volumes. It seems that her daughter has had a real problem with trust.

"My daughter, we will still need his help in this matter. I need you to try and give him some trust for us all to work together." Ravena warned her.

"I trust that he will do his best to help in this matter," was as far as Stella would go in this line of conversation and hoped the Queen will be satisfied with that.

Ravena frowned, nodded her head and was gone. The oval faded away.

Stella dashed to her desk and put the call into her father. She could hear the real concern in his voice as he promised to be ready the moment he was called upon. It struck her odd how time can change one's feelings. When she first met her father she didn't trust him. Now she was forced to trust him, but she can only extend that trust until this problem was solved and hopes that will be enough.

So much has changed for her in just over a year's time. She had denied being part of magic and now not only accepted it but depended on it. It also worried her to realize that she needed Garrett to help her develop her gifts and to train her in them.

Using the magic in her has become easier and easier each time. But she still wanted the human side of her to remain intact. She felt more comfortable knowing that she will always try to do things the human way.

The files on her desk held no interest for her now as she worried about the Fairy World. They lay open on her desk as she thought over everything the Queen said to her. She was so lost in her thoughts that she did not hear the door to her office open. She let out a yelp when a pair of tiny arms wrapped around her, squeezing her.

Deb giggled at Stella's reaction.

The little whirlwind was dressed in one of her own creations today. She had blue ribbons woven through her long blond curls. Her dress was low cut and high riding and looked like it had been dipped in a vat of aqua, blue and teal dyes. She looked like a stormy ocean crashing against the shore. Her three inch spiked heels were dyed the same colours. Stella thought she was only missing the white foamy mist of the seas.

"Wow," was all she could say.

"Do you like it? It's from my newest collection." Deb twirled around making Stella feel dizzy and a bit seasick.

"Does it come with scuba diving equipment?" She goggled.

"You see it. Oh that's wonderful. It's the look I was going for. Water." Deb squealed with delight.

"I would say you nailed it on the head then. You look like the ocean without the spray." Stella laughed at her delight.

"The spray? Oh but of course, you can't have an ocean without a spray. I never thought about that part." Deb bounced up and down, and up and down making Stella's stomach want to pitch from the ocean swelling and ebbing right in front of her.

Stella got up and put firm hands on her tiny shoulders to keep her from bouncing in order to save her stomach. 'God, I should know better than to voice my opinions around her,' she thought.

"So what brings you here this early in the day?" Stella walked over and poured them both a coffee.

"I just wanted you to see what I was working on. I am so excited about this collection. And besides we haven't spent much time together and I was missing you." Her lavender eyes peeked out through thick long lashes brushed blue.

"I'm sorry Deb. I've been kind of busy lately." She offered in way of apology.

"Oh Stella, you're always busy," Deb giggled.

"I thought you would be busy designing your wedding dress and the bride's maid dresses." Stella thought if she brought up the wedding, Deb would fall back on that instead of delving too deeply into her work.

"Oh I've been working on that too. I have my dress almost completed on the drawing board and the bride's maid dresses are still in my head. You and Louise are going to look fabulous." She hugged herself.

"Mm, hmm," Stella muttered as a trickle of fear ran down her spine. She didn't even want to think about what Deb was going to have them wear, it was too terrifying.

"So when is this new collection going to be shown?" Stella hoped getting back to that subject would steer her mind off the wedding.

"Oh, I'm only half way through the designs. It won't be ready for at least a month or so. It is going to be the best one ever, I just know it." Deb bounced again.

Stella brought the coffee cups over to the desk, then wrapping an arm around Deb and led her to the chair. She walked around to sit across the desk from her.

"Well from the outfit you are almost wearing," she laughed, "I can see another hit in the offing." She smiled at her friend.

"Angela is arranging for the backdrop of the runway to look like a waterfall. It's going to be fantastic Stella." Deb hugged herself in glee.

"It couldn't be anything but fantastic, Deb. So how is Richard doing with his new novel?" Stella figured that was a safe subject.

Stella figured mentioning Richard would be a happy subject and was surprised when Deb's little pixie face puckered up in a frown.

"Deb, what is it?" Suddenly she was hit with concern.

"Oh, Stella, he has writer's block and he's so unhappy." Her eyes filled with tears.

Stella got up and walked around her desk to sit on the edge facing her. "Deb, I'm sure that it will pass. He has a lot on his mind right now. He must be thinking about your wedding too and that may cause him to lose some of his concentration. It will pass after you are married."

"You think so Stella?" hope gleamed in her eyes. "Well of course you're right," she rushed on. "Of course he must be nervous. I'm nervous, so he must be too. Once we are married, he'll be able to concentrate on his writing. Oh thank you Stella. I feel so much better. Well, I mean I feel bad for him, but like you said once we are married, his writer's block will go away." Her little pixie face beamed again.

"Yes once you are married and back from your honeymoon, I'm sure he will be able to think more clearly about his book." Stella reassured her.

"I don't understand why this is affecting his writing when it's not affecting my work. Maybe it's just a guy thing." She giggled.

"There you go. That has to be it." Stella laughed. "What is it?" She saw the pained look on Deb's face again.

"I was just wondering how Angela was going to take the change in my designs of putting in the ocean spray into my collection." Now Deb pealed with laughter.

Stella shook her head and joined her in the laughter. No one she knew of could ever keep up with the workings of this genius' mind. And nothing could ever keep this little whirlwind down for more than a few minutes. God she loved her for that and more.

With all that was going on at the time, Stella could have hugged her friend for the distraction. This was only one reason she loves her so much. But life had to be dealt with and her laughter soon died down. Queen Ravena's visit popped into her head sending her thoughts back to the real problems at hand.

Stella was greedy enough not to want to go into the seriousness of life for now. She invited Deb back into her private quarters hoping to take some time to relax and enjoy her friend's company for a bit longer.

Deb was only too happy to go with her. They settled down in her little living room to do a bit of catching up and talk nonsense for a couple of hours.

This felt like the old times where they just hung out together laughing and talking about everything under the sun. Debra relaxed as they chatted and Stella's mind took a bit of a breather from the recent threat and her work.

God it felt good for both of them. Although they both had other friends, Deb had more, but they both knew the friendship they have together was stronger than any other. This was like a mini vacation for them both. They both let go of their problems and just enjoyed each other's company.

Ten

CHAPTER

Celine sat in the first class section of the plane with a glass of champagne in her hand smiling at the thought of a few days in Milan. Oh, but it was really too bad about Johnathan, but it is his own fault really, she convinced herself. If he hadn't started pulling away from me and sneaking around behind my back seeing someone else, and she was sure he was cheating. He wouldn't have had to die. "Is it too much to ask for a little honesty between husband and wife? I gave him some of my best years and never once did I stray from our marriage vows." Celine toasted her faithfulness. Then her eyes narrowed. "You deserve everything you're going to get tonight Johnathan. No one tosses me out and no one cheats on me. I will not be usurped by any of your high and mighty, born into high society women."

Feeling better about the decision to go ahead with the plan, Celine cast her mind to the future and the very good time she was planning to have in Milan. She could envision herself shopping and having extravagant lunches and dining with the elegant friends that she and her husband had accumulated over their few years.

Later that night a dark car with dark tinted windows pulled into the Foxworth's driveway. A tall dark figure got out and walked up to the door. The figure pulled out keys from a pocket and unlocked the front door. No noise came from inside as the family pet Pomeranian had gone missing a couple of days ago so it wouldn't bark and wake up Johnathan. The figure slipped in.

The cops staking the house out watched the darkly clad figure and since no alarms went off they just figured it was a member of the family or a close friend staying there. They figured there was no reason to check out the car or unidentified person since that person gained entrance easily.

Whoever it was that came and gained entry this late apparently didn't come to spend the night. The door opened only a few moments later. The person visiting didn't stay long. They watched the door close and the dark figure climbed back in the car and slowly drive away. Because a stake out is a boring job, one of the cops, the rookie, took down the license plate just for something to do. The rest of the night passed without any further incidences.

The first of the staff arrived at five o'clock in the morning and was soon followed by other members of the staff. Noticing that their shift was almost over, the two cops watching the house decided to call it a night and started the car to leave. Just as they began pulling away, a maid came running out of the house screaming at the top of her lungs. They turned the car around and quickly headed up to the house to the screaming maid.

When they finally calmed the maid down enough, they learned that the Master was dead. The senior cop called it in and then helped the rookie to secure the scene.

George was awakened by the phone ringing. He reached over and answered it. His eyes narrowed as he listened to his detective reporting to him that one of the home's under surveillance was hit and the husband was dead. Johnathan Foxworth was murdered in his bed in the middle of the night right under the cops' noses.

As he dressed, all he could think was that heads would roll. How could this happen when they were right outside the damned house?

Stella woke the same time as George and watched his anger soar. She did not have to ask him what had happened. It was all over his face.

"Who?" was all she said as she hurried to get dressed.

"Johnathan Foxworth." He seethed.

"I'm coming with you," she strapped on her shoulder harness and went down the stairs with him.

"How did they get passed the surveillance?" she asked as they climbed into his car.

"That is the first thing I'm going to ask them when we get there." His anger was riding high. "No one should have gotten past those men."

Stella decided to stay quiet and allow George to concentrate on his driving.

When they arrived, the house was cordoned off and the two cops watching the house that night were standing outside the front door waiting for him.

Stella noticed they were nervous. This was on them and they knew they were in for a good lecture and maybe even a disciplinary action against them. The young cop kept swallowing causing his Adam's apple to bob up and down. Sweat was running down the more senior cop's face. This was every cop's nightmare and it happened to them.

As George climbed out of the car he turned to Stella. "I am going to have to take the statements from these two idiots. I'd like you to go in and see if you can learn anything until I can join you."

From the look in his eyes, she was really glad she was not going to be the one on the receiving end of his anger. She passed the two cops giving them a look of pure sympathy before entering the house.

Even on her way upstairs she could hear George berating the two. When she reached the top of the landing, she made her way cautiously from room to room in search of the Master bedroom.

She smelled it even before she entered. The blood was fresh and soaking the bedding. And there was Johnathan hovering just over the bed where his body lay like a broken toy. She could see the initial stab in his chest and slashes on his arms where he tried to protect himself. The chest gaped open from the stabbing causing the blood to spill out splattering the wall and down his body to pool on the sheets under him. It wasn't a direct stab to the heart but repeated stabbings to the chest for maximum insult and blood loss.

"Uh, hi Mr. Foxworth, my name is Stella Blake." She spoke softly to him and watched his eyes turn from his body to look at her.

"I don't understand." His voice was eerie, his expression showed confusion.

"It's alright Mr. Foxworth; I'm here to help you. Can you tell me who did this to you?"

"I don't understand," he repeated. "How can I be here and down there too?" he pointed to his body on the bed.

"Mr. Foxworth, I don't want to upset you, but you were killed last night. Can you tell me who did this to you?" She tried again.

"I'm dead?"

She knew he was having a hard time processing this. "Yes and I'm very sorry Mr. Foxworth. Please can you tell me who was here last night? Who did this to you?"

"I know I feel strange but I don't feel dead. Is this what dead feels like?" He was caught up in the strangeness of the whole thing and couldn't bring his mind to answer her questions.

Stella was rushed for time. She knew George would be coming soon and had to get some answers from the poor guy before he got there. Then to her utter dismay she heard the tiny tinkling of bells and new Rita was there with her.

"Ooh, cute," Rita squealed.

"Uh, Rita I'm just a little busy right now." Stella's shoulders slumped.

"Oh that's okay, I can wait. Introduce me to you friend Stella." Rita beamed a wide transparent smile. "He's a cute one," she added.

She knew Rita would not leave until she did, so she sighed and looked back at Johnathan. "Johnathan Foxworth, this is Rita Cassidy."

Johnathan looked at Rita and to Stella's total surprise, he perked up and a gleam showed in his eyes. Well as much as a ghost's eyes can gleam. 'Oh God,' she thought, is he really putting the make on another ghost. Okay this was weird and she did not have the time for weird right now.

"Rita don't flirt, I have to get some answers and fast from Johnathan."

"Oh you are always a spoil sport. Okay, okay finish what you were doing and then maybe Johnathan would like to join me and my friends. How about it Johnathan? Would you like to hang with us for awhile?" She bounced sending the bells around her neck pealing.

"Well now, how can I possibly refuse such a gracious invitation?" He bowed to her.

"Mr. Foxworth," Stella's voice was stern now. She was running out of time and patience. "Who did this? Who was here last night?" She demanded.

"I remember I woke up and seen Lauren Wesley here last night. I remember it was strange that she was in my bedroom and then, I am sorry but I really don't remember anything after that." He offered in way of an explanation.

"Thank you Mr. Foxworth. Now I can have a friend come to you. He will look after you and take you where you should be going if you want." She suggested to him.

Johnathan looked over at Rita and smiled. "If it is all the same to you Miss, I think I would like to take this young lady up on her offer," he bowed to Rita sending her into ethereal giggles.

'To each his own,' Stella thought. After all who was she to tell ghosts where they should go. Apparently his personality of a lady's man carried into the next phase of his existence.

"Sure, if that's what you want." She shrugged her shoulders and turned to Rita.

"Make it quick Rita; I don't know how much time I have here alone with the two of you. What did you come to me for?"

"Oh yeah, right, I almost forgot," she went off in more peals of laughter. Then as the memory of what she needed to tell Stella came back in full force, she turned very worried eyes on her. "Remember that air shivering thing that happened awhile ago? Well I'm hearing word that it's happening again and thought I should let you know."

Stella froze. Could Gobrath have found a way to enter her world again? Did this mean he also found a way to create a portal from the Warlock World to the

Fairy World already? She had to get out and find a place to call the Queen.

"Thank you Rita, I'll look into it. I have to go now. You two do whatever ghosts do and take good care of Johnathan." She dashed from the room and passed George on the stairs on his way up. She flew by the officers posted at the door. Diving into George's car she started it up and drove away.

Breaking all speed laws within the city she made it to her office without getting a ticket. For once luck was on her side. Quickly closing and locking the door behind her, she dashed through her office up the stairs and stopped when she reached her living room.

Stella paused to catch her breath then pulled the heat in raising her arms. She felt her hair being freed of the band as the wind slowly lifted her up. Sparks shot from her long green eyes.

"Ravena Queen of the Fairy World, I call upon you to come before me and witness what we do." She waited until a glimmering oval appeared before her and Queen Ravena's face showed in the center.

Ravena's eyes showed concern. "My daughter we have not yet found Gobrath."

"Mother, can Gavin sense the presence of an air shimmer?"

Ravena's eyes widened. "There are many things that my son can do that go beyond our abilities. I will ask him." She disappeared from the large floating oval. When she returned minutes later, she had Gavin with her.

Stella marveled at the beauty of this young boy. His long raven black hair framed an angelic face. He could have been a younger version of his father except for those incredibly deep green eyes shielded under long dark thick lashes. His sweet mouth was turned up at the corners in a smile.

Stella bowed to the young boy watching his smile grow from her show of respect to him.

"Prince Gavin, I am very pleased to meet you." She bowed her head again.

"Stella, you look so much like mother." He beamed at her unable to hide his joy. "I can see that you have the same gifts as I do."

"I am glad that I please you Your Highness."

Ravena bent down to whisper something in his ear. The expression on his face suddenly became very serious.

"Mother tells me you wish to ask me about one of my gifts." His little face looked so grown-up as he spoke.

"Yes Your Highness. It has come to my attention that a portal is being created into my world. I wondered if you could sense it from yours."

"As it happens I have had an odd sensation lately. Could that be what is causing it?" He turned to his mother.

Anything affecting her son went straight to her heart. She pulled her son closer to her and turned worried eyes on Stella. "Is this the answer you seek daughter?" Clearly she was worried for her son.

"Your Majesty I believe what the prince has been experiencing is the attempt at creating another portal to this world." She turned her gaze to Gavin. "Your Highness, do you think you could use this strange sensation to locate the area it is coming from?"

Now that he also knew the reason for this strange feeling, Gavin was more than ready to help in any way possible.

"With the help of my parents and the guards, I could search out the land and see if the sensation grows stronger within me. If that happens then I am sure we will find our answers."

For an eight year old child he responded with surprising maturity. Stella marveled at this young boy's sturdiness and strength. She also noted that Ravena, although extremely worried about the danger to her son, put aside her need to protect in order to allow him to do what must be done for the good of both their worlds. Tears gathered in her eyes as she nodded to Stella.

"Thank you Your Highness. I will get my father to help me search here as well. If we possess the same gifts we should be able to locate it in both our worlds. You are very brave Your Highness." She added and saw the boy's chest puff out in pride from her praise. "Mother I am so sorry that Gavin will once again be facing danger."

"My daughter, my son knows that he is being raised to rule once my time is done. This is what we had all feared since the last time Gobrath attempted to gain entrance to your world. We will leave the palace today to begin our search. I pray that we will all be successful."

Stella watched her fade away still holding her son close to her trying valiantly to stem the flow of tears welling in her eyes.

Stella released her heat when the oval disappeared and floated down to the floor. She took a moment to gather her strength and then banding her flaming glory once more into a ponytail before heading back to George.

He was waiting outside the Foxworth house with a scowl on his face. The forensic team was already at work inside. Tom stood outside taking statements from the officers guarding the door. They shuffled to the side as the coroner's people carried the body out of the house.

When they were both back in the car, George turned to her. "Do you want to tell me what that was all about? And where the hell did you go?" He demanded clearly angry at the way she took off earlier.

"First, I can tell you who killed him and the M.E. will tell you how. But more important we have trouble with a capital 'T' right now. Drive me back to my office and I'll tell you all about it there she ordered." She matched his attitude with her own.

George made good time getting them back to her office. He might not have broken the speed limit like she did, but he made short work of getting them there in a hurry. Stella knew he was fuming but that couldn't be helped at the moment. They had a really big problem that took precedent over any feathers that were ruffled.

Once inside her office, she again locked the door and took her seat behind her desk.

"Okay, Stella, this had better be good. What the hell went on up there in the master bedroom?" His voice boomed shaking the walls.

"If this is the attitude you're going to take with me then you can go to hell and solve your own damned case," her anger was up now. She had more serious matters to consider and being yelled at by him just rubbed her the wrong way.

George was shocked by her attitude. Having her dart from the house and speed away in his car without a word to him caused him some worry. It was simply a knee-jerk reaction to her actions that caused him to raise his voice to her. He always felt he should be the one in control. This stemmed from his childhood, but that didn't register with him at the moment.

George rubbed his face with his hand giving him time to settle down. He knew that he has to apologize to her in order for her to give him the information.

"Stella, I'm sorry, but watching you take off without speaking to me shocked me." He told her.

She thought about his apology and then because her anger stemmed from great worry, she let go some of the anger towards him, not all of it. His domineering and commanding attitude is one thing she can't abide or will ever get used to.

"Johnathan was there," she began calmly. "Lauren Wesley killed him. I couldn't talk him into having Frank take him and look after him." She paused.

"Rita showed up and apparently he liked her offer better."

It felt like his balloon of anger was pricked with a pin. His sudden rage whooshed out and left him empty. He could see by the look on her face that something was up and that look did not hold a happy ending.

"Go on, there's more, I can see it on your face."

'My my, but isn't he in the mood to toss orders at her today,' she scowled.

"Gobrath," was all she said and waited.

George paled and gripped the arms of the chair to steady himself. He knew that Wilfred and his father Geoffrey could not be involved this time. Since she only mentioned Gobrath's name, the trouble must be coming from the other worlds.

"Go on," His blue eyes pierced her.

Stella sat tapping her fingers on the desk and narrowed her eyes at him. His arrogance and attitude was beginning to grate on her. But this is too serious a matter to have a battle of wills right now. That, she promised herself will come at another time. She is finding that his over-bearing and take charge attitude was not something she is going to take much longer. He kept showing her that she is not able to take care of any situation that comes her way. If this is what marriage is all about, having the female cow down to the male, she didn't know if she can tolerate this much longer. She is strong in her own right and got along and did her job before meeting him and knew she can do that again. This thought she will hang on to but not show it at this time.

"The Queen came to me. Gobrath is seeking a portal from her world to his father's and also to ours. Rita saw the same shimmering she saw from the last time he tried. They need our help." She cupped her face in her hands she was so filled with worry she didn't even consider how George was taking the news. This she felt is a problem she must deal with on her own.

For the first time in his life, true fear filled him. His body froze in the icy grip of fear. He sat like a statue not taking his eyes off her face. For a moment his mind shut down. Everything seemed so inconsequential compared to the threat they were facing.

When Stella looked up her heart stopped for a fleeting moment. George had gone into a frozen state. She remembered the last time this happened and knew he was in real danger if his rage began to build. Flames would consume him and he would die.

She bolted out of her chair and raced to him. She took a firm grip on his arms and began to shake him, shake him hard to try to snap him out of it. 'God George please come back to me,' she prayed as she shook him. True fear ran through her veins now as her hands felt the heat building. She had to get to him somehow, get through his mental block. All differences were forgotten now as her fears over him filled her.

Without even thinking about it, she formed a shield around them and put her mouth on his. She pried his lips apart with hers and breathed into his mouth.

Deep down in his catatonic state he smelled her, tasted her scent and slowly, slowly began to thaw until he fell limply back in his chair. Stella held on keeping contact with him until she was sure he was back all the way. She breathed a sigh of relief and sent the shield away.

"Oh God George, I thought I was going to lose you," she laid her lips gently on his again finding them still a bit cool. Then she pressed her cheek against his for a moment to steady herself. She stood up staying close by him until she was sure he wouldn't slide back into that frozen state again then walked around her desk to take her seat.

"I'm so sorry Stella," his voice was a little unsteady still. "The thought of what could happen if Gobrath succeeded filled me so full of fear I couldn't feel anything else."

"I know my mind just wouldn't let me think of that. I guess I just concentrated on how to stop him. The Queen is searching for him and George," she paused, "she has to allow Gavin to help."

Tears welled in her eyes at the thought of that beautiful child being put in harm's way.

"I know that is tearing her heart in two. He is so beautiful and so sweet just like his parents. If anything happens to him I couldn't bear it, even knowing that his death would result in a domino effect in our world. We won't even exist if he is killed."

"Stella, the Queen and Prince will see to his safety at all costs. Tell me what she said and the plans that have already been made. What can I do to help?"

Again he was issuing orders to her. But this is so important and dangerous that she has to let that ugly feeling go for now.

Stella went through the plan to have Gavin use his gift to seek out the spot where the first portal is being constructed. Then she told him how they plan to hold Gobrath in a combined binding spell while the Queen and the Prince perform an erasing spell that will make him forever forget how to create a portal.

"So we have to hope that they come up with the spell by the time they find Gobrath and have the three of you bind him. That's putting a lot of faith in everyone." George frowned knowing this plan had little chance of working.

"Yeah, I thought of that too. It depends on them finding him before he completes the spell to open the portal and us binding him and also finding the right spell to erase his memory." She joined him in a frown of her own.

"We know that time and space is irrelevant when it comes to all three worlds, but timing will be the factor for success or failure. It's a mess."

"I don't see that there is anything we can do but have you and your father checking for the portal here, while I finish up with the murder case until you need me."

"I'll call Rita and get her to use the ghost hotline or whatever the hell ghosts use to communicate with each other. They can do a search probably faster and wider than we can. Garrett is waiting for my call to start our search."

"Then I should let you get on with that and I'll go back to the precinct to work on the case." He wasn't happy that his powers were not called for to help her. It made him feel useless and not needed and less than what he is.

Stella sensed what this was doing to him and wished that she could find a way for him to join in, but Warlock powers were not enough for this task. Even though he is the most powerful Warlock on earth, she and her father had powers above and beyond his. It broke her heart to feel the hurt he was feeling.

"George you know that it was you that dealt with Geoffrey and his son and it was you that captured and dealt with Glenda. You have saved me so many times because of what you are. I'm sorry that this time different powers are needed to stop Gobrath. I will need you when everything is in place."

George felt foolish to be jealous of her powers. "Stella, it's just my ego getting the better of me. I realize that there will be times that my powers won't be enough and I just have to come to terms with that. I love you with all my heart." He got up went over to her and kissed her gently. "Let me know how you make out and I'll let you know how this case is going. Call your father," he said as he walked out of the office.

As George drove back to his office he thought over their conversation. He knew deep down that this threat needed more than he has to give to it. He also knew it is going to take some time to come to terms with the fact that his powers alone will not be enough at certain times. This is a blow to his ego. Before Stella found out about her heritage, he felt that he was the strongest Warlock on the Earth. Now he has to bow down to his wife and her father having more power than he possesses. This is going to take considerable time for him to come to terms with and accept. He reached into his pocket for the button he always carried and rubbed his thumb over it. To him this brought Stella closer to him.

Stella didn't like the fact that George and the squad were going to take over the case she was instrumental in gathering the right information on. Before meeting him she was the one to always see all her cases to their close. Ever since they met things have changed for her and she was never one for welcoming change. The biggest change is allowing him to take over because he is now doing the job she held. Although she has come to the decision that she doesn't want that job back, she is having a very hard time with him stepping in and taking over just because he is a member of the Force and she isn't anymore.

Stella felt that she is going to have to think this whole thing over once she gets the time to do that. Losing even an ounce of control is not something she thinks she can stomach or deal with.

ELEVEN

L auren sat at her vanity preening herself. Oh she felt so wonderful. It was like having been filled with a special power. Her thoughts turned to her own husband and how very soon she would be rid of him and be able to keep everything she had worked so hard for.

As she brushed her hair with her pearl handled brush, she went over the events of last night and knew she left nothing of herself behind. Even the borrowed car could not be traced back to her. She felt all powerful.

There was only a fleeting moment where she thought maybe she couldn't go through with it, but after killing him she felt like a Goddess. It was a new found powerful feeling. My God but it filled her with such euphoria and power, it was intoxicating.

Lauren began to think that maybe after the plan she and her friends had agreed to was fulfilled, she just might go into the assassination business. It was very clear to her that she had a real penchant for it, the personality and talent. Her mind went back to the moment she drove the knife into Johnathan's chest and it felt god-like.

She stood over him watching the life drain out of his eyes sending a thrill and not a chill up and down her spine. Now she wondered why she had let the other women do it instead of her.

Bertrum walked into her dressing room just as those thoughts raced through her mind. He saw the smile on her face and once again congratulated himself on choosing such a sweet compliant wife. He absolutely adored her.

She had been a wonderful help to him in his business dealings and with his many health problems. She was always helpful and sympathetic to his needs. There was nothing he wouldn't do to keep her happy. He loves her with all his heart.

Bertrum walked over and placed a kiss on the top of her head. "Darling you get more beautiful with every day that passes." He murmured.

Keeping the smile on her face she accepted his act of devotion all the while wishing he was already dead and in the ground.

"Thank you my love," she kept her voice tender.

"Life would be perfect if only Fritz hadn't run off. I really miss that crazy Terrier." His smile dimmed just a little as he stood behind his wife.

"Oh, now Berty, don't you fret. I'm sure he'll come back and look very sorry for running off like that. You just wait and see." Her smile brightened, but it wasn't for the hope of the dog's return. She was thinking about the day she took the dog for a drive and threw him out in the country side two days ago.

Bertrum laughed, imagining the friendly Terrier walking up to him head bent down in apology to him. "You know I don't think I can bring myself to discipline him when he does come home. I miss him that much. Maybe just a light scolding will do."

"That's right darling," Lauren reached up and patted the hand he laid on her shoulder. "Now I have to finish getting ready for the day." She returned to fussing with her hair. "And you are going to be late for your golf date." She reminded him.

"Oh, that's right," he checked his watch and moved away to change for the game. "I'm running a bit late, but not to worry I know they will hold the tee for me." He called over his shoulder.

Stella called her father. As soon as she hung up the phone he materialized beside her.

"You really have to show me how to do that." Her eyes gleamed with anticipation. She knew that she will have to rely on him to show her some of her gifts and how to use them.

"I will but at another time," he smiled at her. "Right now we have serious work ahead of us."

"Garrett you are a direct descendant of Gavin, so if he has the gift to sense a shimmer in time and space, I wondered if you have the same gift."

"I have many talents as do you. If as you say Gavin can sense that, then I see no reason we can't do the same. I know I am older and have had longer to hone my talents, dear, but I believe you possess all the same talents that I do. We will have to concentrate and hope that we are able to sense the shimmer." He laid a comforting hand on her shoulder. He just wished that she would call him Father instead of his given name. This shows him that she still has not come to fully accept him yet.

"Okay, we need to figure out a search pattern and I do have some help in that area." She grinned.

"Rita," she called out.

They both heard the tinkling bells just before Rita appeared. She wasn't alone this time. She brought along her new friend Johnathan.

Garrett although surprised, was also pleased with his daughter's acceptance at using her gifts.

Rita's face lit up, as much as a ghost's face can at the sight of the incredibly handsome man standing beside Stella. She began preening herself and batting her eyelashes at him. Rita could not help being a big flirt. It was part of her personality that still clung to her in her after life.

"Oooh, Stella, who is this absolutely delicious specimen of man. Hi, I'm Rita Cassidy," she introduced herself and giggled.

"Rita, this is Garrett Stone," she turned to him shaking her head, "Garrett, Rita."

Garrett bowed to her causing her to giggle even more. "I'm pleased to make your acquaintance Miss Cassidy." He turned to Johnathan, "And who is your charming friend?"

"Oh, this is Johnathan Foxworth," she quickly glanced at Johnathan. "He's new to my way of life. I'm just showing him the ropes so to speak."

The men exchanged greetings. Stella noticed that Johnathan looked a bit confused during all this.

"Okay Rita, now that the introductions are over, I called you here for your help." She made her voice stern to get her full attention.

"Garrett and I want to set out a search pattern for that shimmer you said you heard about. I need you and your friends to do a sweep and if any of you see it or feel it, come find me and tell me where right away."

"Gotchya," Rita bounced sending the bells around her neck and dangling from her ears ringing. "Oh Johnathan," she turned to him, "this is going to be so much fun. Working with Stella is always an adventure and a blast."

It seemed Johnathan was still trying to find his bearings and only nodded to Rita. Right now everything was confusing for him but he did enjoy the company of this vibrant girl with all the bells on her.

When they finally left, Stella and Garrett got down to the business of pulling out maps and forming a direction for their search. They both knew it was a long shot and since neither of them had sensed the shimmer before, they only hoped that they would be able to do so this time. The worlds depended on them finding it before Gobrath completes the spell that will open the portal allowing him to enter this world.

They folded up the maps and Stella packed them in her bag then they headed out the door to begin searching. A long shot was better than nothing and it was all they could do. Both of them hoped that Gavin, Ravena and Gareg were having better luck in their world.

Louise was sitting at the kitchen table in the Manor with all the Blake women discussing the shower plans. They were thrilled at the suggestion Stella made for the theme. Now that the theme was set, they could get down to finalizing the details.

The date was set. Angela was on-board arranging the venue like a fashion show. Her mind was whirling having two venues to arrange since Deb's real fashion show was scheduled soon.

Louise had booked the ball room at the Belvedere. Maria and Wanda were putting together the menu to be catered. Gwen and Morgana agreed to help Angela with the decorations.

The large table was strewn with invitations, envelopes and lists. As Louise talked about the shower, the Blake's tried not to let on or show the worry they all felt about the danger that was coming. They knew that Garrett had gone to Stella's to help deal with that.

"It is going to be wonderful. Oh I just can't wait to see Deb's reaction when she walks in and sees it." Louise's face beamed with joy. "This is going to be the absolute best shower we have put on yet."

"Yes, I think Deb will be thrilled with it," Wanda said trying to keep her voice light. "Louise you have done a marvelous job organizing this whole thing. I know that Stella is very grateful to you for taking charge. If she wasn't so busy right now, I know she would have loved to play a bigger part in the planning."

"Stella is always busy Wanda," Louise couldn't hide the disappointment she felt in Deb's best friend.

"Yes I know and it really is a shame, but really she can't help it. People depend on her to help them Louise." Wanda stiffened at the affront to her daughter.

"Wanda, her friends depend on her too, but she always finds an excuse not to be there for them."

Wanda's eyes narrowed. Gwen could see a battle coming on and sent a wave of calm through the room. With the real danger lurking, they didn't need to start a fight here among themselves.

When everyone seemed to calm down, thanks to Gwen, they settled down to fill out the invitations in silence from the list of names on the table.

Louise's conscience nagged at her until she finally had to apologize to Wanda for her outburst. She had always felt there was something about this family, something different. But it was just plain bad manners to chastise a member of it in their own home. Sometimes her anger got the better of her.

"I apologize for talking about Stella that way, Wanda. I do know that she is busy and people do depend on her to help them. I just wish that she had more time to spare for her friends and family is all I meant." She said softly.

"Louise," Gwen piped in. "she is very busy and yes strangers do depend on her for her help. But she is always here for the family when we most need her. It hurts her too, not to be able to put more time in on the shower arrangements. Trust me Louise, I know my sister."

"I'm sorry Gwen. I don't have sisters or an extended family like this one so I guess I really shouldn't have said what I did. I apologize again." Louise hoped her statement would help mend the hurt feelings she caused Wanda.

"Oh, pish-posh," Morgana huffed. "We are here so let's get busy and get this done. Besides," she added, "if Stella was here, she would just pick a fight with Gwen and we'd get nothing accomplished." She laughed causing her voluptuous bosoms to bounce up and down.

That brought out a smile in them all.

Morgana put everyone back on track and she too felt better when they all got busy with the various details to be worked out. But in the back of her mind, she couldn't help but be worried about the bigger problem facing their family and this World. So much depended on two Worlds working together to save them both.

Gobrath was in the Fairy World sitting in his latest conquest's home very pleased with himself. It was only a matter of time now before he can bring his Father King Gorkin into this World and together they will find a way to enter the Human World. All three Worlds will then belong to them and they will rule them all.

He can't wait to see his brother annihilated by their Father. Neither he nor his Father tolerated weakness and Gareg showed that quality in spades. With him out of the way and the Fairy Queen and that offspring killed, there will be nothing to stop them ruling all three Worlds. Once that happens he has his own secret plan to get rid of his Father so he can be the sole ruler.

After all, his father rules their World and has for centuries. It's time he took his rightful place as ruler. Being King of all three Worlds filled his mind and boosted his already outrageously enormous ego. Gobrath saw himself ruling all subjects of all three Worlds with an iron fist. Once he accomplishes this and destroys his father, no one will ever tell him what to do or say from then on or they will suffer the penalty of death after he enjoys their screams from being tortured. This is what he is really looking forward to. This is what his father has taught him.

What he didn't know is that the Queen has contacted the Human World. He felt that all his actions were protected and concealed from the Royal Family in this World. In his own mind he felt he was very clever in the way he set out to destroy them all, especially is brother and eventually his Father. All three Worlds will belong to him and he alone will rule them all.

Gobrath could not help the laughter that spilled out thinking he has finally found a way to take charge and win the battle over all three Worlds. To him the Queen of the Fairy World was so weak that she didn't even contemplate that her World is at jeopardy at the moment. Gorkin always told him that the Fairy World was weak and now he believed him. Ruling should never be left in the hands of women, they are too weak in his estimation.

TWELVE

George was having his own problems. He knew who killed Johnathan Foxworth but couldn't tell his team. Lauren had left nothing for forensics and the license plate was a rental, rented in the name of one of Wesley's employees. He looked around at his squad's dejected faces.

"We can't help the fact that we set up the stake-out late and that the victim's wife never gave away her plans to go on vacation to anyone, which we know of." He added. "We'll have to chalk that up as a mark against us and go on from there. The stake-out will continue round the clock. If another one of these women leave unexpectedly we'll move in and get the spouse to agree to a guard inside the house. According to the list we have, there are still more targets out there."

"I'm still burned that that idiot cop didn't have the brains to do his job. A rookie, for God sakes, had more sense and wrote down the license plate." Sally fumed. "If he had done his job and checked out the car sooner we might have caught the perp. I mean who the hell gives out a key and the codes to your home to a company employee, for God's sake."

"Detective Pride I assure you that the seasoned officer will never make that mistake again." George's eyes went to steel showing his own rage at the sloppy, incompetence of a senior cop.

"He is currently doing his penitence walking a beat until I feel he is qualified to once again join the mobile units. That I can guarantee won't be for years." George was still seething over the stupidity that Officer showed.

If that was the look their Lieutenant gave to the idiot they felt certain that his blood must have turned to ice in his veins. They had all seen the tip of his anger before and never wanted to see what lay underneath it. At that moment they all felt that the idiot cop got off lucky just to be alive.

"Then we're back to bloody square one," Tom interjected.

"Not square one, Tom. We do have a list of possible victims." George leaned forward in his chair. "I think it would be a good idea to pay our respects at the funeral. Since it was a homicide, no one should be surprised to see a bunch of cops there. We can observe everyone's reactions while keeping a low profile."

Celine was notified and on her way back from Milan. She had just checked into her hotel when Lauren called her to tell her the news and to be ready to put on a sad face. It wasn't long after Lauren called that the police tracked her down to give her the terrible news.

Sitting in first class, she could drop the façade kick off her shoes and be herself. She sipped champagne and toasted her good fortune. She would take the few hours on the plane to relax before she was forced to put on the act of a lifetime.

Hours later, when her plane landed she was met by the police and escorted to the morgue to identify the body of her now dead husband. She had practiced the tears and had them flowing on cue like a river. Anyone watching her would see how devastated she was.

When she was driven home, her maid told her she had a lot of calls from her friends offering their condolences.

"I don't want to talk to anyone right now," she told the maid.

She kept the act and the tears going until she reached the safety of her bedroom. After closing and locking the door, she jumped around hugging herself.

She was free and rich. Everything was working out perfectly.

Rita kept popping in periodically to report that so far none of her friends have found the shimmer yet. She gave the locations of their searches and went back to continue the search.

She and her father were having no better luck either. Stella wondered, not for the first time, that maybe they weren't detecting the shimmer because Gobrath may be busy with something else for the moment. After all, the Queen has sent out a search party and he most likely got wind of that. If he is not actively attempting to open the portal, there was no shimmer in the air to detect.

An idea struck her and she called for Rita.

"Hey Stella," she grinned. It appeared that Rita was finding this whole thing an exciting adventure.

"Rita, can you tell us where the shimmer was?"

"Well I didn't see it. A friend of one of our gang saw it and reported it to us." She explained.

"Did that ghost tell your friend where he spotted it?"

"Well yeah," she bounced sending the bells tinkling. "It was just north of the city, but he said it's not there now."

Stella looked at her father. They had started their search west and were on a pattern that would take them clockwise in the area. Now that she had some kind of direction, she knew they had to abandon that plan and head north.

While they drove, Stella could not rid herself of the memory of the look of fear on Betty's face. Although she knew she was safely guarded and that the Wesley's had no idea of the true reason she has not come in to work, she worried that Bentley may not be able to keep a composed face around his employers which might give him away.

Just as those thought were going on in her head, she rounded a corner and her cell rang. "Yeah," she answered it swerving around to pass a particularly slow moving vehicle in front of her.

"Miss Blake," Bentley's voice whispered on the other end. "I don't know if this is important but I thought I would call you to tell you that I witnessed the Mistress leaving the house last night. And Miss Blake," he pause for a second. "I found her attire very unusual."

"How late do they have you work Bentley?"

The time of the murder was after midnight.

"Oh, I wasn't on duty at the time Miss. As it happened, I could not remember locking up and got up from my bed to check. That's when I saw the Mistress coming down the stairs and watched her turn off the alarm and walk out of the house. It appeared that I did indeed lock up before I retired. Miss Blake it was the way she was dressed and acting that I called you about."

"How was she dressed?" Stella knew but this was gold if George could get him to testify to it.

"Well she was dressed in a sweater and slacks. They were black and she was wearing a dark woolen cap. The outfit was definitely not her style. I found it very strange. And she was wearing dark low heeled rubber soled shoes. I noticed that she kept looking over her shoulder as she made her way down the stairs and tip-toed out the door. All this was very much against her normal behavior. It worried me so much that I just had to call you and tell you."

Stella had pulled over to the curb by this time. Bentley didn't know it, but he was giving her a good piece of evidence that would help put his Mistress away for a very long time.

"Bentley I need you to do something for me."

"If I can Miss," he agreed keeping his voice low.

"I need you to find an excuse to leave the house and go to the police station. Go up to the homicide division and ask to talk to Lieutenant George Smale and tell him exactly what you told me."

"Oh Miss, this is bad isn't it?"

"You want to keep Betty safe Bentley, you have to do this."

"You really think my Mistress is involved," she could hear the turmoil in his voice. He was battling with his loyalty for his employers and the real danger to the cook.

"I think you know the answer to that Bentley. This is no time for you to back out now. Your Master's life could very well depend on your decision."

"Of course," he didn't hesitate once she mentioned the danger to Mr. Wesley. "I'll make some excuse and go down there within the hour.

Stella pulled away from the curb and continued to drive north taking them out of the city and heading to London.

They drove all day and came up empty. Even Rita's group reported that they couldn't find the shimmer. Both Stella and her father realized that Gobrath must have gotten wind of the search and was lying low for awhile.

She dropped her father off at the Manor and headed home. She found George in his home office going over notes from his case. They had found a pattern of the murders. There was a murder every two weeks according to his detectives' notes. Since the last murder was committed last night, they had two weeks to work the case before the next one was scheduled.

George looked up from his notes the moment she walked in the doorway. "Bentley came to see me today. Thanks Stella. The statement he gave will go a long way to putting her away for life. But we both know that she did not commit all the murders. That's quite a group of women with a lot of vengeance in their hearts."

"I don't care what's in their hearts," Stella stormed. "No one should be allowed to go around killing for any reason, and just to keep a lifestyle you've become accustomed to is absolutely NOT a good reason."

"On that we both agree," he smiled at her and looked at his watch. "We'd better go down, I'm sure cook has our meal all prepared by now." George got up and draping an arm around her took them both downstairs to the dining room.

The meal was delicious as usual, but Stella's mind kept going over the events of the day. She knew that Gobrath had stopped the spell on the portal. He must know that everyone was looking for him. If only they could get the female he was courting to tell them where he was working, they could find him faster. She knew the female was being interrogated by the Queen's men. Since no word has come to her, she had to think that maybe Gobrath kept even that a secret from her or has wiped her mind of that information.

Her mind whirled with the fact that they couldn't locate the portal. So far Gobrath has been too smart for them. Her biggest worry was that Gavin was putting himself in direct danger. If anything happened to him life could change in an instant, not to mention that it would devastate the Queen.

The next morning, Stella picked up her father and continued the search. George went to his office to prepare his squad in what to look for at the viewing at William's Funeral Home.

After paying their respects to the grieving widow they were to casually walk away and position themselves in strategic places to get a better view of everyone that came through.

They would attend the funeral the next day as well. But today might give them a sense of all the players. Since the group of women that met weekly for lunch would most likely be closer to each other than the rest of the people coming for support, they would get a good look at them and how they reacted to each other. That was exactly what George wanted his squad to see.

He wondered if any of them knew about the stake-outs on their homes. This murder was committed with cops sitting right across the street. For some reason that did not register with the murderer as she drove right by them to do the deed and drove by them again when she left without batting an eye. They had been given special instructions to blend in and not be spotted by anyone.

George gave special orders to his men to keep a particular eye on Mrs. Wesley at the funeral home.

Figuring he knew what he was doing they all agreed, but didn't like the fact that he was holding back some information from them.

The lines formed. Hands were shaken. One after the other people offered condolences and heartfelt sympathy to the widow. She greeted each one with sorrowful eyes and thanked them for their support and kind words.

George marveled at the superb acting job Mrs. Foxworth was putting on. Had she chosen acting as a profession, she would have won an Oscar for the role she was playing today, he thought. He could not stop his eyes from narrowing when he glanced her way.

Tom was stationed on the other side of the room across from her. He had a bird's eye view. He pretended to sip coffee from a Styrofoam cup as he kept her in his sights. She spoke to everyone in turn as they came up to her, taking their offered hand accepting the support, dabbing at her eyes with a lace monogrammed handkerchief adding to her performance. He did notice that with some of the women, the corners of her mouth lifted slightly as if holding back a secret. Tom took mental notes of the women that brought out that reaction from the widow. One woman, she actually smiled at as she accepted her condolences.

'The L.T. is just never wrong,' he thought to himself. In that respect he kind of reminded him of his old L.T. Then he gave himself a mental shake. Of course, she was married to him and he would talk to her about the case. He wondered if it was her idea to watch certain people a little closer. Now he could not hide his own smile the thought of that brought on. He took a sip to try and hide the involuntary smile. After all this was not the kind of place one should be standing around smiling.

When it was getting close to the time for everyone to leave, George signaled for his squad to take off and head back to headquarters.

Back at the station, he called his squad into the conference room to go over their observations. Each report came up with the same people that they felt were of particular interest. George checked the names of those against the list he had and decided to take off a couple of the stake-outs. That left them with only four homes to cover. It narrowed it down nicely. Each detective stated that Lauren Wesley was of particular interest. They all noticed the other women on the list had treated her like some kind of leader. While all the women greeted each other cordially, they showed a slight difference in the way they acted when she was with them.

"Well I think it's plain that we found the ringleader of the pack," Sally trumped up.

"Yeah, well you hit the nail on the head with that one boss." Tom gave a mock salute to George. He felt it better to keep his thoughts to himself how he thought the boss came up with the ringleader.

George looked at him and a corner of his mouth lifted. He knew exactly what Tom was thinking. If only Tom knew it wasn't a hunch his wife had, but the statement from the victim's ghost that gave her the name of the murderer. And of course he could not tell any of them that.

"Since all of you are in agreement that Lauren Wesley is the ringleader of this little women's group, we have our work cut out. There is no evidence to point to any of them for these murders. We have to catch them in the act or as close to it as we can in order to put an end to this rash of murders."

While George carried on with his team planning their next course of action, his foster sister Louise was at the Belvedere running through the planning of the shower with the wait staff and manager. Morgana opted to join her. Wanda was just too jittery having Garrett away from her, and she had had about enough drama in that house for awhile. Having a man bent on murdering her son-in-law staying in her home earlier and now this horrific problem has run its toll on her. That was the last case he and Stella worked and thankfully solved.

They had a pleasant time organizing the way the food would be served, the menu to be prepared and placing the table seating for everyone. Louise was in her glory and her imagination was running wild.

The raised runway had to be constructed yet, but she could envision it as she glanced around the room. Convincing all the Blake women to walk down it like professional models was another thing. Of course they would be wearing their own style of dress for the occasion. Now it dawned on her that she had to have a spokesperson to describe the clothes each wore before coming out of the end of the runway.

"I know Angela is doing so much for us and doing her job for Deb, but do you think she would mind being the orator for the event too?" She asked Morgana.

"From what I have seen so far, there is nothing she would not do for that sweet little girl." Morgana smiled at Louise.

"We will owe her big time for the extra time she will have to put into this event." Louise hugged herself. She could just see the whole thing come to life in her mind. "Oh, Morgana, I just know that Deb will be so thrilled with all the details of her shower."

"When is Angela coming to put the place in order?" Morgana asked.

"She said she could come over for two nights before the event. She was so happy and so full of ideas. I know she will make this a huge success."

"Then I suggest that all the women taking part in walking down that runway should pick out their outfits and tell Angela what they will be wearing so she can describe them like a real fashion show," Morgana suggested.

"Yes, yes, you are right Morgana. If you can ask your family, I'll select an outfit and call Angela and maybe someone should ask Stella what she is going to wear." Louise was so excited about this part of the surprise for Debra.

There was nothing more to do. The venue was planned. Angela was scheduled to do the decorating. The menu was selected and the wait staff had their orders. The invitations were sent. By the weekend it would all be in place and Deb would have the shower of her dreams.

Suddenly Morgana froze where she stood. She saw the slight shimmer in the air. Her reflexes took over and she sent a pile of paperwork sitting on a table to suddenly slide off and scatter on the floor. Louise quickly ran over to pick them up off the floor. Morgana pulled out her cell and put a call into Stella immediately.

Morgana quickly but quietly explained to Stella the phenomena that she just witnessed. "Stella, I believe that Gobrath is casting his spell. The air just made a shimmer here at the Belvedere in the ball room."

"Morgana, we are too far away. Get Louise out of there as fast as you can and I'll contact the Queen." Stella ended the call and pulled over quickly.

She scrambled out of the car and dashed down a deserted alleyway. Garrett raced after her. Calling the Queen meant that Stella had to transform too; she could not do that in the confines of the car. Garrett quickly cast a spell to conceal them if anyone should happen to come along.

"Ravena Queen of the Fairy World I call upon you to come before me and witness what we do." She cast the ancient spell.

Stella floated above the ground, the wind she created swirling around her loosening the band on her hair so her flaming glory blew around her face. A jewel edged oval appeared before her. The Queen appeared inside it almost immediately.

"My child what is it? We have not found him yet I am sad to report."

"Mother, I have just heard from my cousin. I believe Gobrath is attempting his spell again. The Belvedere is Northwest in my city. My cousin saw the air shimmer there."

"Then we will seek in the Northwest. Thank you my child and I beseech you to take every precaution. I will come to you again once we have searched that area. Wish us all good fortune my child." She disappeared and the oval faded away.

Garrett looked at his daughter. He could not have been prouder of his daughter. The way she did not hesitate to use her gift showed him she was growing in her powers.

Back in the car, Stella sat behind the wheel drumming her fingers on it. She would have preferred the battle to be somewhere more private than inside a building. How were they going to do a magical battle in a building where there were hundreds of people at any given time?

She finally turned to him. "Garrett how can we fight him there?"

"It matters not where the battle will take place my little one," he laid his hand on her cheek. "We have the power to conceal what we do. Let us hope that they find him so we can bind him and that our ancestors can come up with the spell to erase his memory."

Stella had forgotten that the Queen had yet to come up with the right spell. The binding they put on Gobrath the last time did not last as long as they wished it to. She feared for the young Prince.

"Stella," Garrett knew he had to get her thoughts off what she could not control and they had to get to the Belvedere as fast as they could. "We have to get to Morgana."

Even though fear filled her, she knew her father was right. They had to get to Morgana as quickly as possible. She shook her head to clear it and drove like a maniac back to the center of the city to the Belvedere.

Morgana, in the mean time convinced Louise that everything was done that could be done for now and suggested that she go on home and relax for awhile. She convinced her that she could look after all the minor details for now. Louise was reluctant but gave in gracefully and left her there.

A half hour later, Stella and Garrett walked into the ballroom to find Morgana waiting for them. Her face was pale and they saw that her nerves were on edge. She was sitting down staring at the space where the shimmer occurred. It looked to them that she feared if she took her eyes off of it, it might disappear on her. When she heard there voices, all she did was point to a spot in the room.

THIRTEEN

Stella and Garrett walked over to the spot Morgana pointed to. Garrett's eyes sparked when he drew closer. Stella felt a small shiver run up her spine. She always attributed that to her tingles, but now she wondered if it also had a different meaning to her.

Garrett watched her and saw the reaction. He smiled at her and nodded his head, showing her that he was pleased her gifts were getting stronger.

"It was definitely here Morgana," Garrett turned to look at her and noticed she still kept her eyes on the spot. He wondered if she expected it to appear again.

Suddenly a horrible thought occurred to Stella. Her face paled. "What if we can't do this in time? What if the Queen doesn't find him and he tries again when everyone is here for the shower? Oh my God, what will we do then?" Stella's legs gave out and she slunk down to sit on the floor.

To her surprise, her father stood there looking down at her and bent over laughing.

"How can you laugh at this?" Stella screamed up at him as she watched him grab his sides at the uncontrollable laughter coming out.

"As much as I have seen and heard about this adorable little creature that you are all putting the shower on for, I think she would be absolutely over the moon if there was an extra bit of entertainment at this event. She might even think it was all part of the program put on for her benefit."

Stella stopped and thought about what he said. Knowing Deb like she does, that is exactly what she would think. Then she too started to laugh uncontrollably.

Morgana was having none of this nonsense. This was a serious problem and not one to be laughing about. She raised her plump body out of the chair and putting her hands on her rounded hips glared at them both.

"I do not see the humour in this situation. What I see is a very big problem that must be solved, and solved quickly." She bellowed at the two tear-stained faced pair howling with laughter. "Now get your sorry asses up off the floor and start taking this seriously."

Garrett reached over and helped the two of them up. Morgana's anger had the laughter die down, but they were still grinning as they stood looking at her.

Stella was the first one to gain some semblance of control. "I'm sorry cousin, you are right. This is a very serious matter. But I don't see what we can do right now. The portal is not being worked on at the moment and the Queen has not gotten in touch to tell us that Gobrath has been found. We still don't know if they have come up with the right spell yet. What would you have us do?"

"Well I wouldn't have you laughing, that's for damned sure." Morgana huffed, obviously very angry with the pair of them.

"My dear Morgana, you have shown us where the portal is being created and that is something we didn't have before. It all depends on the Queen for the time being." Garrett straightened himself up and spoke with a commanding voice. "Until she can locate Gobrath all we can do is monitor this area to see if he will try again."

"What can we do? There has to be something we can all do until the Queen contacts Stella again." Morgana's fear was peeking though.

"We have Gwen," he said softly. "She can use her mind to keep an eye on this spot and warn us if the portal opens again. Without the Queen's help from her side of things we can only watch and wait."

"But if he succeeds," Morgana whooshed out through her fear.

"Then Gwen will see and Stella and I will come immediately and bind Gobrath. Let us all hope that is not necessary, but if it is hopefully we can bind him in time for the other's to perform the spell."

"So much is depending on the Queen finding the right spell," Morgana shook her head. This plan had so many things that could go wrong with it, like the Queen not finding the spell and Stella and Garrett not getting to Gobrath in time. She could not remember the last time she felt fear like this in her entire life. She had never felt such fear before. As a rule she was the one that kept the family grounded with her no-nonsense reasoning. This is beyond her abilities and that has her worried the most. The one thing she didn't want to happen is to lose her clear and logical thinking like her cousin Wanda always does in times of crisis. Weakness of any kind is abhorrent to her. She had that in common with her young cousin Stella.

There was nothing more they could do for now. Garrett told Stella he would take Morgana back to the Manor with him so she could head back to her office and do some work to take her mind off the problem for now.

She watched him put an arm around Morgana's large shoulders and then they were gone in a blink of an eye.

Oh she really had to get her father to show her how to do that, she thought as she headed out to drive herself back to her office.

Stella's mind was reeling with all the responsibilities she was taking on. Instead of heading straight to her office, she found herself driving aimlessly around the city. It helped her to run though all the facts and to put them all in order. It gave her a sense of what should be the next step in the problem. As her mind was doing that, she found herself near the clearing of the woods behind the Manor.

Deciding on some fresh air, Stella climbed out of the car and walked towards the clearing. With her mind so full, she did not see how the trees circling the clearing were bowing in her direction as she passed them. A strange sound penetrated her concentration. It was like a thousand voices speaking at once in hushed tones. She couldn't make out any one particular voice or the words that were being said.

She stopped and stood still. Fear gripped her, like icy cold fingers, holding her, preventing her from moving. It felt like the first time she saw what a Warlock could do to a human. It filled her with so much fear she couldn't breathe. Her eyes darted everywhere trying to find where the voices were coming from. When she caught the strange movement of the trees swaying and leaning towards her, and there was no wind to cause such actions, her breath caught in her lungs.

"Garrett," she did not know at that time if she just thought the word or spoke it, she was so terrified.

Arms suddenly wrapped around her startling her so much it snapped her out of her frozen state. She screamed at the top of her lungs. Then she found herself suddenly being whirled around and coming face to face with her father as the ear splitting screams continued to pour out of her.

Garrett pulled her to him burying her face in his chest to muffle her screams. The scent of him slowly penetrated her senses and she wrapped her arms around him clinging to him as if her very life depended on it.

Although his face was pale at witnessing the state of his daughter when he appeared, he soon realized what caused her to be so afraid. He rocked her gently in his arms until he felt her breathing slowing down enough to feel safe in easing up his hold on her.

"Stella, my child," he lifted her chin up gently. "Tell me what frightened you."

Her eyes were still glazed with residual fear. "Voices," she whispered. "I heard so many voices all whispering around me but I couldn't see anyone."

"It was because there was no one whispering, darling. It was the trees speaking to you. Look," he turned her to face toward the edge of the clearing.

All the trees were still gently swaying and bowing in her direction. "But trees can't talk. Maybe it was a group of ghosts that I just can't see." She worried maybe her gift was failing her.

"Trust me Stella, it was the trees. It's part of the gift you and I share. We can communicate with all living things." He grinned down at her.

"I can hear trees talking? They can talk? But I've never heard them before." She turned a puzzled face up to him.

"Your gifts are growing. It could be because I am here and we have found each other. You have always had the gift but didn't know it. Had you believed from the start about our blood line, your gifts most likely would have manifested themselves earlier to you."

The incredible look on his daughters face brought out a deep laughter of joy from him. His daughter was coming into her true self and it was wonderful to watch. There was so much more for her to discover about herself and he will be there to show and teach her. He could hardly wait. But right now the trees were trying to tell her something.

"Stella, I want you to stand here and close your eyes. Concentrate on bringing only one voice into your head." He knew the trees had the power to talk to one or more at a time and right now they only wished to communicate with her.

She did as he asked and taking a leap of faith closed her eyes and concentrated on listening. A rush of hushed voices bombarded her mind causing her to sway. Garrett caught hold of her arms to steady her. Sweat beading on her forehead with the effort to latch on to only one of the voices.

"Help us. Help us, the time grows short. The black is coming from far away. We heard them planning to destroy us all. The Coven must help or we are lost."

Stella's eyes flew open revealing sparks forming behind her long sea-green eyes. The strength behind the pleas for help had heat instantly build in her causing her to transform. Garrett jumped back as the wind around her picked up in speed and strength lifting her. The band holding her ponytail flew off and her red flame of hair swirled around her head. She grew and grew until she was as tall as the trees that were whispering to her. Instead of the shirt, jacket and slacks she wore, she now wore a startling white gown that flowed out around her body. A jeweled band criss- crossed her breasts. She lifted her arms and brought thunder and lightning to crash around them. A sparkling jeweled crown now adorned her head.

Her voice boomed out. "Who has threatened the life of the forest?" She demanded.

Suddenly the tips of the surrounding trees bowed until their tops reached the ground. The grass and bushes shivered. Swirling thick clouds built over their heads, as lightning bolts lit up the skies above them.

"We do not know her name," one of the trees whispered. "We only know she is close to the Queen. Her heart is cold as stone. We heard her talking to the dark Prince."

Garrett fearing for his daughter, transformed to be at her side. His dark blue-green eyes shot out sparks. His thick black hair swirled around his head in their combined wind. A crown did not form on his head. They floated above the ground like enormous Greek Gods. Even though he could not hear the trees' side of the conversation, he felt he needed to be by her side.

"Tell me at once what you heard them say." She ordered.

The trees whispered among themselves and then all but one lifted themselves to once again stand erect. The one left bowing low to her was delegated to give the information. The rest all stood shivering where they stood.

"Your Highness, we heard them speak of betrayal. The Dark Prince ordered the woman to stay close to the Queen and persuade her to look in all the wrong places. The Dark Prince assured her that the time was near and they would soon rule all the worlds. He also told her that if she could not sway the Queen in the wrong direction, she was to murder the young Prince."

The vile anger that consumed her hearing of the plan to harm the prince had the skies open up and lightning fill the clearing scorching the ground. She reached up and called the sun to come into her hand and was about to cast it down when Garrett grabbed her.

"Stella," his voice resounded over the noise and made the earth shake beneath them, halting her from destroying the clearing. "Think of what you are doing. Take your anger and use it against Gobrath but do not use it to destroy this place." He commanded her.

Flames shot out all around them from her anger. Her green eyes were hidden from all the sparks shooting out of them. She imagined Gobrath and sending a lightning bolt through his black heart. The piece of sun burned red hot in her hand as she looked down at it. She couldn't stop the image in her mind of sending it flying at that monster.

Since she was unable to do any of those things and her father had a strong grip on her, she brought her thoughts back to the present and realized she was hurting the vegetation around them. Slowly her anger began to fade away.

She sent the piece of sun back to where it belonged and began to release the heat within her. They both floated gently down to the ground and she collapsed. Garrett sat beside her, cradling her in his arms until her strength returned.

When the colour came back into her face he lifted her chin to look into her eyes. "What did they tell you Stella?"

"I'm sorry Garrett, but I think I only want to tell it once. Come with me and I'll drive us back to the Manor. I'll call George to come and meet us there."

It still bothered him that she refused to call him father instead of his given name. This again showed him that she has a very hard time in trusting.

Gathered around the kitchen table, Maria made the tea before taking her seat. Everyone waited for Stella to speak. She told them everything the trees told her. It was a long drawn out moment before anyone managed to shake off the shock of the news.

"You have to tell the Queen." Wanda was the first one to speak.

"Yes," Stella agreed. "I should have contacted her already, but I wanted everyone here to know first. I'll tell her now." Stella stood up and took a few steps back from the table.

She brought in the heat to call to her Queen. "Ravena, Queen of the Fairy World. I call upon you to come before me and witness what we do."

The oval ring appeared almost immediately. Inside it, the face of their Queen appeared wearing her crown. "Daughter, what news do you have?"

Stella floated in the air before the oval ring and told her everything the trees told her. Her heart broke knowing she was telling the Queen that a trusted friend has betrayed her. She saw the hurt in the Queen's eyes.

"I know the one of which you speak my child. After you gave us the direction, one of my lady's maids tried to convince us that was the wrong direction. She is the cousin of one of my dearest friends."

Anger shot out of Ravena's eyes at this betrayal and the threat to her son. A plot against the royal family was punishable by death. This punishment will be carried out immediately. Ravena turned her head to issue out the order to bring the maid to her.

"Mother, please try to find out everything this young woman knows. If she can tell us how much time we have, it will help us." Stella pleaded.

"You have my word that this person will be put through a thorough inquisition before I order her punishment. Thank you my child for warning us and again saving the life of my son. We will of course continue our search in the direction you gave us."

"Mother, how close are you to finding the spell?"

"We are still working very hard on it and I can tell you that I do believe that we are very close to finding the right one."

"That is good news mother. Thank you."

"Be safe my child."

Queen Ravena left with a determined look in her eyes. The oval ring disappeared. Stella released her heat and floated down. This time her energy did not fade as she took her seat.

"What made you go to that clearing Stella?" Morgana asked.

"What? Oh, I don't know. I was just driving around trying to line up all the facts in my head and found myself parked near it. It was just a fluke that I got out of the car and wandered into it."

"No," Garrett smiled. "It wasn't a fluke, but part of what you are that took you there."

"You think so dear?" Wanda smiled at Garrett and then Stella. Nothing pleased her more than to have Stella accept and develop what was in her.

"I believe that her gifts are coming to her faster and easier now." Garrett smiled back at Wanda. They were two very proud parents.

Stella didn't know what to think about their attitude towards her now. She still could not give her full trust to either one of them. Not really knowing this man that sired her and having her mother show herself as a traitor still resonates within her. Her mother rushed to his side after the dream she had of Garrett standing over her family lying dead on the ground.

FOURTEEN

Clark Kent had decided to play hooky from school for a few days. If he was going to be a top notched reporter, he felt he needed some real field work. Since he did some of the research already on the computer and had most of Stella's notes on the case and privy to the crime board she had put up, he knew that Lauren Wesley is what the police call a woman of interest.

He decided to do a little checking on his own. Clark packed his backpack with binoculars, a camera, notebook and pens and a few snacks just in case it took longer than expected. He left a note at home saying he was meeting friends after class so his mother and father wouldn't worry about him.

Considering his backpack had everything he'd need, he took himself off to where the Wesley's lived and to find a place to hide and wait. He spotted the police surveillance set up and ducked into some bushes out of sight. It was only due to the fact that he knew about the surveillance that he spotted them. It did indeed amaze him how well they blended in. No-one not knowing about them might not have made them.

Clark took out his binoculars and notebook. He settled down to watch the windows of the house for now. For a few hours he was able to watch the service staff go about their business. A few times he caught sight of Lauren and her husband going about doing theirs.

He watched as Bertrum climbed into his chauffeur driven town car and drove away. Since he carried out a suitcase and his briefcase, Clark assumed he was going on a business trip. That left only Lauren to watch.

About an hour later, when he figured there was no point in hanging around, since it looked like she was not going anywhere, Clark began to pack up his gear to leave. He had just closed the flap on his pack when a car drove into the laneway. Clark quickly pulled out his binoculars and wrote down the license number. Then he watched as Celine Foxworth climbed out and was ushered inside the house by a butler.

He recognized Celine by her picture in the paper when it ran her husband's murder. Uncomfortable and hungry, he had already eaten his snacks earlier, Clark decided to hunker down and stay a bit longer. Another car pulled in and another woman got out and was ushered inside the house. Soon the laneway began to fill up with cars, each carrying a single woman.

'Well, well,' Clark thought to himself. 'Looks like a meeting is being held right here as well.' Now he wondered if he should just wait around taking notes or should he call Stella and tell her about this. He was sure that the surveillance across the street was taking notes as well. 'Good thing he took pictures of each woman,' he thought.

There was really nothing Stella could do at the moment even if he did call her, so he decided to wait until all the women left and then give her the list of license plates. If he could run them himself, he would do that before notifying her, but since he knew the DMV would not give out that information to him, he would have to give them to her. He would download the pictures and give those to her as well.

The meeting lasted for hours and it was getting late when the women filed out one by one and drove away. Clark was hungry and thirsty by now. "Damn, why didn't I think to bring more supplies with me?" He cursed his oversight. He waited around for another hour and when nothing further happened, decided to sneak away.

When he got clear of the house and the surveillance, he pulled out his cell phone and called Stella.

She was waiting for him in her office by the time he got there. She held out her hand for his notes and he could see she was angry.

"What the hell do you think you were doing? Going out there alone and skipping your classes. You broke our agreement Clark and you put yourself in danger." Her eyes pinned him where he stood. "You could have been arrested or worse. Do you think for one moment if those women knew you were there they wouldn't put you on their list for murder?" She took his notes and stomped over to her desk.

"I did what any good reporter would do." His voice cracked.

"Well you are not a reporter, not yet. And you can thank your lucky stars that you weren't caught. You will not put yourself in danger again as long as you work for me. Do you understand?" She barked at him and watched his face turn red. "How on God's green earth do you think I could tell your mother that you got arrested or even worse, killed while working for me?"

"I just did what you would have done," he tried to explain himself.

"I'm a licensed Private Investigator with over a dozen years on the police force. You are a student." She bluntly reminded him. She knew her anger stemmed from fear of the danger he put himself in but couldn't help it.

Being put in his place brought out his own anger. "I'm not an idiot and I'm not a kid. Yes, I'm a student and I asked to work for you because you are the best and I thought I could learn more from you than a stuffy classroom. I did not get caught by them or the police and I got information you didn't have before. I also took pictures of every one of those ladies entering the house."

'Well, he's got spunk,' she thought. She sat back in her chair and stared at him. "This time everything worked out okay, but from now on, if you want to continue working for me, you tell me what you are going to do before doing it or we can end this association now."

Clark blew out a breath. He thought for sure she was going to kick him out. He realized she was giving him a second chance and he would die before admitting to her that he was scared to the bones all the time he sat in those bushes.

"Okay," he breathed out.

"Good," now give me those pictures," was all she said and began to run the plates he had written down in his notebook.

Clark just stood there not handing over the pictures.

"I said hand them over," Stella commanded.

"Before I do anything you need to realize that I'm not a kid but a man and I won't be scolded by you or anyone. Yes I'm attending college and that means I have some brains. I can go to the police with what I have since I can't go to the newspaper under the confidentiality contract I signed. I came to you to learn, but that doesn't mean I will be dictated to or that I haven't learned a few things in my classes. I give you a lot of respect and I don't think it's out of line to ask for some of that back." He was royally pissed at the way she spoke to him.

Having him speak up to her in this fashion had her sitting back in her chair. She knew she only ranted at him because of the fear she had of him being hurt or worse killed. But to listen to him stand up to her this way forced her to realize that she didn't show him respect as a man or a person.

"Clark, I apologize for my outbursts. Telling me what you did scared me to death that you could have been hurt. You are a man and yes I agreed for you to learn from me. I would appreciate it if from now on that you inform me of any future actions you wish to take on your own." She hoped to placate him. "Now please hand over the pictures so I can run them and add them to the file we have on them." She was really amazed at the way this young lad stood up to her and kept his ground. It was as though he transformed from mild manner Clark, to Superman. His parents should be very proud of him.

Clark stood there still angry, but he eventually handed over the pictures to her.

Stella knew even before she ran them that they would turn out to belong to the women on the list of the luncheon friends. She also knew that the police watching the Wesley property would have done their run on them too. George would already be informed of who visited Lauren this evening and the length of time they spent there.

For him to threaten her of taking them to the police was irrelevant because they would already have this information, and that was something he didn't think through, but to stand up for himself like he just did put him up a few notches on the golden ladder of respect.

Stella knew that anyone that went to so much trouble to plan out a series of murders and taking such care as to not leave any evidence must have it documented somewhere. If only she could get into the Wesley home without anyone seeing her, she could find it. At this time there was no cause for George to get a warrant issued to search her house.

She had to admit that Clark did well. He was beginning to think like a real reporter but he was still green around the gills yet and could get hurt. She also knows that she is being pulled in too many directions right now to be affective in any one of them. If only she could figure out which husband was next on the hit list, she could end this investigation and put her full concentration on the more important one, Gobrath, the younger son of King Gorkin of the Warlock World.

It didn't take long for her to get the complete list of names to the license plates. She got up and added those names with the picture of each one Clark gave her. She drew arrows pointing to the ring leader, Lauren Wesley. Taking everything else off the board she stood looking at it and decided to match the names of the deceased to addresses on a map. This might give her the clue as to which husband was up next for their little meeting of revenge.

She circled the addresses on the map and drew lines linking them. When she was done, she stood back and stared at the map. There was a pattern forming. The lines formed from the left side of the map in a backward slash and the beginning of a forward slash almost creating the shape of a V. Checking the other names sure to be targets, Stella drew broken lines and when she finished it was a clear W. "W, for Wesley?" she wondered.

According to her figuring, the Maxwell's were next on the list. If she was right, she now knew the next target and because each hit was done in a bi-weekly timeline, she knew the timing. It was time to call

George and hand it over to him. As much as she hated to give over a case, she just had more important matters to deal with.

George knew he had two weeks to save Cliff Maxwell's life if the women stuck to their schedule. Because he did not want to take a chance on any of the other men's lives, he kept the surveillance on them all but had his squad pay particular attention to the Maxwell's home.

To keep his squad from forming any ideas about him, he decided to let them in on what Stella told him and how she came to her conclusions. It might grate on their ego's a bit to know that a student of journalism helped her to reach her conclusions. That was better than them trying to find out more about him.

Their feathers were ruffled seeing how a mere student got more information than the police did with all their resources and training, but they were professional enough to take this new information and do their jobs. The only saving grace for them was that they knew there wouldn't be another murder attempt for another two weeks. At least they got to breathe a little easier until then.

"I have to ask myself," George announced to his men, "since a student was able to stake out the Wesley's without any of you knowing and get the same information you all got, how is it that Stella can find a pattern in the killings and none of you did." He glared at them.

They all had the good grace to bow their heads in embarrassment.

"Lt.," Tom spoke out. "I'm ashamed that we didn't think to line up the facts and murders to apply them to a map once we got all the information from our stake-out. This is one mistake that I can assure you will never happen again."

"For God's sake Detective, she trained you all. I would think that you could put that training to good use. Don't let this ever happen again. I don't like the fact that someone outside the Force, including my wife, can do the job better than us." George bellowed.

For their Boss to talk this way about his wife told them how disappointed he was in them. This was another burden for them to bear and they needed to show him that they can do the job. From now on they all felt that they will follow the training and show him that they can do the job they were all trained to do. This showed them all that they must be getting lazy and that has to stop.

"We won't let you down again Boss," Bob stated for the squad and saw them all nodding their heads.

This time they all left the meeting determined to solve the case and do their jobs the way they'd been trained. They just learned that they had all forgotten the training they received from their old boss and now it was time to remember all that training a put it to use.

Stella had a hard time letting go of the case. It was never in her nature to do so. Gobrath was just too important and she knew she needed all her attention to deal with that problem. Something was nagging at the back of her mind. She felt she was overlooking something and needed her full attention to find out what that was.

Until she dealt with Gobrath, and God she hoped they will win this battle, there would be no more new cases. She told Clark to go home and she would call him when she started a new case.

Of course he thought it was some kind of punishment for his rash behavior getting sent home and not allowed to come back until she called him. He packed up his gear and with his head down, stormed out with a dejected air.

Stella couldn't worry about his hurt feelings right now. She had to think and think hard. There was something she was overlooking and it was important. In her mind, she retraced all the steps and facts so far concerning Gobrath and his plan.

The trees told her she needed to bring in the Coven. That's what she forgot. Oh, that was going to be a treat, she thought. She picked up the phone and called Maria.

"What's wrong darling," her mother's voice panicked on the other end.

"Mother, nothing is wrong. I need to talk to Maria. Is she around?" She knew her mother would know she was worried.

"Well of course she is around. Where else would she be? You're worried about something, I can see it." Wanda insisted.

"Mother, we are all worried about the situation we're in. Please, mother I need to ask Maria to do something for me." Stella beseeched her mother.

"Oh, very well, if you don't want to tell me what's wrong," Stella heard the hurt in her mother's voice. Then Maria was on the line.

"Maria, I need you to ask Gertrude to go to the Coven and ask them for their assistance. We need them to fight with us."

"I can ask Stella, but you know how the Coven feels about Gertrude and Tempest. They may not be very cooperative." Maria felt compelled to explain.

"If she puts it to them that they would all be destroyed along with everything else if Gobrath succeeds maybe they might change their minds." Stella fumed. She was so glad that she wasn't a Witch and didn't belong to a bunch of old ladies with narrow minds.

Maria sighed on the other end. She knew Stella could never understand the life of Witches and the total dependence they have on their Covens, the need for it. A Coven is home and family and protection to a Witch. Leaving a Coven was like severing a limb. She knew Gertrude and Tempest were suffering greatly from being cast out.

"I will talk to Gertrude and ask her to speak to the Elders Stella, but I can't see them wanting to help her or us."

"Maria, I can't tell you how I know, but if we are all to survive we need them."

"Then I'm sure Gertrude will do her best to convince them of this."

When Stella hung up, she sat back closed her eyes and hoped with all she was that Gertrude would be successful. While her eyes were still closed, a thought came into her head. She sprang forward in her chair. Her eyes flew wide open.

"Location," she spoke out loud. "How could the shimmer have occurred in two locations, one north and one northwest?" That was the missing link that she missed. Then it hit her like a lightning bolt. "He isn't creating a portal, he is creating multiple portals. That's why they can't find him in the Fairy World."

Stella jumped out of her chair and dashed to the middle of the room. She began to bring the heat in to call the Queen when the door burst open. The surprise of that happening had the heat whooshing out of her.

"Oh don't you look silly," Deb bounced in. "Why are you standing in the middle of your office with your arms up in the air?" She giggled.

'Not now,' was all Stella could think, and then found herself embraced in a bear hug. Deb clung to her like a tight girdle cutting off her air. It took some strength, but for self preservation, Stella finally managed to wiggle out of the skin tight embrace and looked down at a very vibrant pixie-like looking woman.

Her blonde curls were done up in sparkling strands of material framing her little pixie face. Those lavender eyes glowed with delight. Her little heart shaped mouth was turned up at the corners in a sweet smile. The rest of her was gowned in one of her latest creations that only Deb could pull off and look adorable in.

"I love you to death Deb, but if you keep insisting on squeezing the very life out of me, I may not be around for your wedding."

Deb giggled even harder. "Don't be silly," She began bouncing around the room on her three inch spiked heels.

"I don't find a bunch of broken ribs funny, you idiot," Stella smiled as she started patting her ribs to make sure they weren't actually broken. For such a little thing she was as strong as an ox.

"So what brings you here when you should be hip deep in your fashion designing work?" Stella walked them both to her desk and plunked her friend down in a chair.

Before she could take her own seat, Deb shot up again and started bouncing where she stood.

"It is done. I'm finished. I just had to come over here and tell you that it is the most wonderful collection in the whole wide world. It is the best thing I have ever done." She hugged herself while spinning and bouncing.

Stella's eyes began to spin in her head watching her. She grabbed hold of her desk to keep her from keeling over. 'God,' she thought, 'she's like a tiny powerful tornado.'

She closed her eyes. "Deb sit," she ordered. "If you keep spinning like that I'm going to puke all over."

Deb giggled even harder.

"Oh don't be silly," but she did sit down. Then her lips turned down in a pout. "Angela kicked me out of my own studio."

Now it was Stella's turn to laugh. She could just envision her acting like she just did and Angela, worn out, exhausted from all the work she'd been doing, wanting only peace and quiet for a bit and tossing out the whirlwind to get it.

When Stella finally managed to get herself under control, she noticed that Deb didn't take kindly to her laughing at her problem. "I'm sorry Deb, but you have to admit that you can be over the top with your enthusiasm sometimes. I'm sure that Angela didn't mean to hurt your feelings. She's just probably exhausted from doing a good job for you." Stella could not wipe the smile off her face.

Deb cocked her head to the side and thought about what her friend said. "Maybe you're right. She did do a wonderful job. I get so caught up in what I'm doing that I don't take time to think how hard she works." Now that she thought about it, it made sense the way Stella explained it and her smile came back.

'God nothing keeps this woman down for long,' Stella realized again. But then no one could ever keep up with the goings on in her little genius brain. It seems all thoughts simply flit in and then just as quickly flit out except for the ones about designing. Those thoughts seem to be the only ones that take hold, take root and remained.

After sitting down and watching the emotions play out on her friends face, Stella had to wonder how this little bundle of energy and 'out of this World' ideas could attach themselves to her down to earth simple way of life. She was an enigma to say the least, but Stella could not imagine a life without her.

"Angela will do anything for you, she adores you," Stella told her.

"Oh and I love her so much too. But you're right, I do work her far too hard, but oh Stella, I just can't help it when I get these really terrific ideas I just have to see them come to life." Deb peeked through her lashes at her.

And because she was talking about her ideas, she couldn't help going into all the details of what put the ideas into her head in the first place. She raced on describing her new line of clothing.

Stella's brain was sent into a whirlwind at the constant chatter her friend was famous for. Everything left her mind as the barrage of words blurred coming out of that tiny heart-shaped mouth. It ended up sounding like 'blah, blah, blah, blah,' like a Peanuts cartoon.

She began to fear that she might never be able to understand another conversation from anyone ever again. Stella's eyes glazed over as her friend kept up this incessant chattering.

There was no stopping Debra once she latched onto the topic of her designs. Stella marveled at the energy bottled up in one so tiny. Even Dolly Parton was no match for this little tornado. She was sure of that now.

God she loved this energized friend, but this was definitely the wrong time for her to be sitting here listening to the entire goings on of her mind. Once Stella was faced with problematic cases or magic, she just could not give her full attention to the rattling on from her friend.

FIFTEEN

I t really was good to see Deb again but it just happened to be the wrong time to visit. In order to protect her sanity Stella's mind drifted to the important matter at hand and only gave her friend short answers accompanied by nods and shakes of the head.

The lack of real interest did not go unnoticed on Debra Styles. When she finally realized she had lost her audience she stopped talking. Deb cocked her head to the side and waited. It took a few minutes for her friend to realize the room was silent.

"Oh, I'm sorry Deb," she apologized. "I had other things on my mind."

"Do any of those things have anything to do with me finding you standing in the middle of the room with your arms up in the air?"

"In a way, I guess I was just frustrated and threw my arms up," she offered as an explanation.

"And you can't tell me what it is because it has to do with your work. Right?" Deb pouted. She knew Stella never talked about a case she was currently working on.

"Yes it has to do with my work, sorry Deb."

"Well then, since your attention is not on us, I should let you go so you can get on with it. I just wanted you to know that my collection is finished and that it is the best thing I have ever done." Deb got up.

Stella rose up out of her chair and went around and put her arm around her friend as she walked her to the door. "You say that about every collection you've done and you are right every time." Stella gave Deb a hard one arm squeeze.

"It's true, I do," she giggled. "I hope you can finish this case you are on soon so we can have some real time together before the showing."

Stella watched her go and felt sorry that now Deb was being kicked out of two places. But then, knowing Debra, she will bounce back in no time.

Left alone, Stella locked the door and walked to the middle of the room to call the Queen.

"Ravena Queen of the Fairy World, I call upon you to come before me and witness what we do." She floated above the floor and waited for her Queen to appear to her.

They talked a long time. Stella told her about her fears that Gobrath was creating more than one portal. She saw that this news worried her Queen. Splitting up was not an option if she was to keep her son safe. The biggest worry had to do with what would happen to all three Worlds if more than one portal was opened at the same time. The laws of physics and nature might not tolerate such a breech. If that was the case, all the Worlds would be in peril of being destroyed.

"My daughter, this is terrible news. We have found the spell to erase his memory, but if we are not in time all our efforts will be for nothing."

"Mother, you must catch him at a portal that he opens and contact us at once. Let us all hope that this can be done in time."

"I have instructed all Fairies to join in the search. I am saddened that I cannot at this time trust any of my other subjects. Pray we find him in time."

When they finished, Stella released her heat and lay limp on the floor.

She let out a scream when she found herself suddenly being lifted up off the floor and held in a pair of very strong arms. The scent of her father shot through her senses and she relaxed.

She looked up at him as he carried her across the room. "Why are you here?" She asked as he gently set her down in her chair.

"I felt your distress." He smiled down at her.

"You have got to teach me this Garrett. Her eyes were wide in wonder.

"We will begin your lessons once the World is safe again. I promise."

To stop hovering over her, since he noticed it made her feel edgy, he took a seat across from her. "Now tell me what happened to put you in such distress." His brow wrinkled sending his eyebrows to pull together.

Stella took a deep breath to calm herself down first. "I called the Queen. An idea struck me and I had to talk to her about it."

"What was this idea? Can you talk about it?" he knew sometimes the Queen issued what is known here as a gag order.

"Yes, and everyone should know. I believe that Gobrath is creating more than one portal to our world. He might be doing the same to the Warlock world as well." Just speaking of it again had panic running through her like a vicious river.

"Calm down, sweetheart," Garrett felt her panic hit him like a fist.

Stella took a couple of deep steadying breaths before continuing. Once she felt her system slow its' quacking she leaned back and shut her eyes for a moment.

She opened her eyes and spoke more calmly. "The Queen fears that if more than one portal is opened at the same time it would have a devastating effect on all three Worlds." She paused.

"Queen Ravena said they have completed the spell to use on him once he is located and bound. That was the good news."

"Now tell my why you think there are more than one portal being created?" His mind was trying to work out the logic in what his daughter was telling him.

"You remember me telling you that Rita said one of her ghost friends saw the shimmer."

"Yes, that's what alerted us all." Garrett agreed.

"Yeah, well then Morgana saw another at the Belvedere and the trees in the forest told us they saw one too. Three different places witnessed by three different entities. That must mean there is more than one portal. That is at least three different ones here from that information. I can't help but wonder if he has as many started from the Fairy World to his Warlock World as well."

"I see the logic in it and yes I agree with your analysis. This is indeed a problem." He rested his elbows on the arms of the chair raising his hands and began tapping his fingertips together.

"There's another problem Garrett." She was tapping her fingers on the desk. "The Queen refuses to divide the search party. She fears for her son if they split up. She is calling the Fairies from her world to help in the search."

"Stella, nothing must happen to Gavin or it will affect all of us. I can understand and agree with her decision in this matter. We, on the other hand can split up and search. I feel the best way is to have all three sightings covered and hope they are the only attempts at portals to our world."

Relief washed over her. Just talking it over with her father and listening to his opinions on what should be done lifted the heavy burden off of her shoulders. She had never shared her responsibilities with anyone before, nor did she want to before, for obvious reasons. But now it felt wonderful not to be the sole bearer of this burden. This problem was just too big for any one person to handle alone.

Everything depended on team work working in sync. Two worlds had to coordinate and cooperate in precision like a well oiled machine.

"Garrett I will need you to go back to the Manor and tell everyone the new development and set up the arrangements with everyone for each location."

"I will do that, but first I believe I was wrong, the time has come to learn how to transport. You may need this power for this battle."

Stella's eyebrows winged up disappearing under her bangs. Excitement grew and spread out through her. So many gifts have come to her without her willing them recently, but this is one that has not manifested itself yet and she was dying to learn it.

They worked hard for a couple of hours. Beads of sweat formed on her face from her efforts. By the time Garrett called an end to the lessons, she had managed to transport herself only a few feet. But to her it felt marvelous. It was like winning the grand prize. She was still beaming with a wide smile after he left her to go back to the Manor and tell the family the news of the portals.

Wanda was not as pleased as Garrett had hoped. He thought that her daughter's achievement would be welcomed with a great amount of pride in her daughter. What he found was her finding another reason to worry for her.

"Garrett, she is not ready for this. You have accepted all your life what you are and what you are capable of doing. Stella is your offspring but she is like a newborn babe with all this magic. This could be too much for her to take in. She has just come into the realization of what is flowing inside her." She worried.

"Wanda you do her an injustice." Garrett tried to soothe her. "She has accepted and she is doing all she can to adapt to what she is," he tried to convince her. "She is stronger than you think."

"You have not been here while she grew up my darling. She has denied what has flowed in her veins all her life. It is only recently that she has been forced to come to terms with what she truly is. I don't think she is strong enough to face what we are up against." Wanda pleaded her case.

"Darling, you are right in saying that I have not been here for her throughout her life. I am here for her now and I can tell you that she is up to the challenge that this family is facing. Because of our love, I am asking you to trust me with our daughter," Garrett spoke gently to the love of his life.

Just the look he gave her and the determination of his words, Wanda had to give in to him, trusting that he would keep her daughter safe.

SIXTEEN

L auren greeted the other women before taking her seat in the dining room of Chez Francois. It was their weekly luncheon. She was absolutely glowing. Her new found talent filled her with excitement.

Seated at the table were the three widows and four yet to become widows, including herself. A couple of the women opted out of the meeting saying they just wanted to enjoy their new lives now. The widows sat with a smile, while the others kept glancing around nervously. It struck her funny the different reactions from the group at her table.

"Ladies," Lauren called the meeting to order. All eyes suddenly turned to look at her.

"I think we should all order and then we can discuss our plans over our meal."

Three of the women who had already got their wish shrugged and nodded their heads. The other three nodded but fidgeted with their jewelry or napkins.

Lauren noticed their nervousness and knew that others in the dining room would as well if they did not get themselves under control. With the feeling of power running through her veins, she found her patience with them was growing dim.

After the waiter came, took their orders and left, she leaned forward and spoke in a hushed voice.

"Get your selves under control," she spoke between gritted teeth. "Look how happy Celine, Brenda and Colleen are. Do you want to stay miserable and worried or do you want the peace and security they have achieved?" She glowered at them. "I'm telling you right now if you let your nerves get the better of you and have people notice it, we could all spend the rest of our lives in prison instead of living the good life."

The three women stopped their fidgeting immediately. They all glanced at the three women beaming. The waiter returned with their orders, set them down and left.

The three widows ate with enthusiasm, whereas the other women picked at their lunch. Lauren shook her head at them and dove into her food. She found her senses heightened ever since she killed Johnathan. Food tasted better, the air and flowers smelled sweeter, the world looked brighter. It was exhilarating.

She knew they had better get their conversation done before finishing the meal and having the waiter come back to remove the plates.

"Now I know Barbara that you are up next to gain your freedom, but I would like to beg a favour from all of you." She stabbed an artichoke and put it in her mouth. She took her time chewing and savouring the flavour before swallowing.

"Bertrum is away for an overnight business trip. I would like him to be next. I was thinking that this could be accomplished tomorrow night if that is okay with everyone."

They had all drawn names at the beginning and Barbara knew she drew Bertrum's name. She choked on a piece of asparagus. Celine reached over and tapped her on the back to help. The asparagus dislodged and she swallowed. She took a sip of wine to help it down.

"Oh," was all she could manage.

Lauren couldn't help herself. She began to laugh at the pure terror on Barbara's face. When she finally got herself under control, she looked across the table at Barbara.

"Part of that favour is that you allow me to do the work Barbara." She was stunned by the total relief that washed over the woman's face for not having to carry out her part in it.

"But our plan is that the wife is out of town Lauren." Celine banged her cutlery down on the table. "If you are around the police might suspect you. Why are you changing the plan when it's working so well?"

"I have my reasons Celine." She did not want any of them to know the thrill she got out of killing a human being or that she was thinking of going into the professional assassination game.

"I'm sorry Lauren but we cannot agree to this." Celine looked to the other women and thankfully got a nod from them all.

Lauren felt like tossing them all out on their ear, but she knew if she pressed the matter, they would suspect her of something. The disappointment was overwhelming. Then she thought that maybe if she went along with them, she might be able to convince them to let her do the rest of the murders. That was something she had to plan out very carefully in order to get her way.

"Very well, but I do want Bertrum to be next. I'm sorry Barbara but you are up to bat tomorrow night."

"We always wait two weeks Lauren." Barbara's voice came out in a forced whisper.

"Yes and that is setting a pattern for the police. A pattern could catch us up. We need to break the pattern to take the suspicion off of us."

The women took a moment to think of this and when they saw the sense in it they all agreed. If they kept to their pattern, the police might stake out their houses and catch them.

Lauren had come up with this plan and its' worked so far. They were sure she must be right about this too.

Lauren saw it in their faces that they were agreeing with her.

"Alright, I'll pack a bag and head to our country home tomorrow evening. She pulled out her spare key and code and handed them over to Barbara.

Once the business part of the luncheon was finished, they all relaxed and continued on with lighter conversations. Lauren could hardly contain her joy thinking she would be free from that doting husband of hers very soon. God, she was bored of his constant pawing and sickly sweet flattery.

While the ladies all kept up their chatter, Lauren was thinking of her soon-to-be freedom. She envisioned herself living free to do and be what she should have been born to do and to be, instead of being born to moderate income parents scraping to get by.

It was the day for meetings. They were being held all over the city, the women at Chez Francois, her family at the Manor and George at the precinct.

"We have to close this case fast." George looked around at his squad. "It appears we are draining the budget with all the surveillance we've set up. I've just argued the time frame of the murders to Brass and we have exactly two weeks to get the job done. After that, we have to pull off the stake-outs and no more over-time."

"But we're damned near positive who is behind it. Can't Brass stretch it just a little longer?" Tom's anger peeked through.

"Trust me Tom, I argued till I was blue in the face. He won't give us any more time." George held a grip on his own justified anger.

"If we could just find a way to make this murdering bunch of women step up their time table, we could end this in the time frame Brass has given us. Maybe we should just write them a nice letter and ask them to help us out with that." Sally said sarcastically.

"Yeah, wouldn't that be the cherry on top," Bob scoffed. "We'll tell them that Brass gave us a time limit on catching them. Or better still, why don't we ask them to simply stop murdering their damned husbands."

"Okay, okay," George put up his hands to stop the flow of pent up anger spewing from his team. "We have two weeks so let's use it well and get the job done in that time frame."

"What else can we do?" Tom demanded.

"We keep at it. We keep our eyes and ears peeled and hope to God they make a mistake." The last thing George wanted was to see his team deflated with their frustrations. "You all have all the facts now so get out there and get the job done." He bellowed.

They all knew he was talking about the information Stella provided. Now it was up to them to finish the job.

"We have the surveillance set in place still so let's just hope they spot something that will lead to an arrest. You all know what to do. You have your assignments, so get out there and do your jobs." He dismissed his squad on a note of frustration.

George heard the mumbles from all of them as they dragged their feet out of the office. If only he could use his magic to end this, he thought. He knew they had to solve this soon or this case could break their spirits. But damn it all to Hell, Stella provided them with information that should lead them to ending this. If they didn't, he was faced with a very sad duty ahead of him. He will have to search and find one or more to discipline or transfer out of his Department.

As soon as the last one left, his phone rang.

"Homicide, Lieutenant Smale," he answered.

"George, we need to talk," He heard the urgency in her voice.

"I'll be right there," He hung up and rushed out of his office. The sound in her voice had him racing through the squad. He never noticed their heads whip up as he flew past with surprised looks on their faces, or the hope shining in their eyes thinking that their LT just got a hot clue to their case. The one thing that didn't strike them was the fact that if it is a clue sending him out, then why didn't he call them all back into his office first to inform them? This is one more showing of their lack of ability lately to deduce facts.

George made it to her office in record time. He rushed in the door and found Stella sitting quietly behind her desk. He skidded to a halt when he didn't find her in danger but sitting very calmly. For some strange reason seeing her like that worried him even more.

"What's happened Stella? What's wrong?" Something inside him told him something was very wrong.

"I've asked Garrett to fill in the family at the Manor. I thought I should fill you in here." She rubbed her face. "Sit down George, please."

He walked over and took a seat across from her. His senses picked up the panic running through her even though she sat giving a quiet air of calm. Fiery heat began to burn in him readying his body for any attack. His eyes turned to cobalt as the heat built.

"Stella, for God's sake what's wrong? I can sense something is causing you to panic. Tell me so I can help you." His voice shook the walls.

Stella's hands flew down to the desk and when she saw his reaction, she raised them up palms out. "There is no danger here George, calm down." She pleaded.

George refused to let go of the heat until he was sure. "Explain," he demanded.

"Yes, yes, okay, just calm down. The danger is not in this office. This danger threatens the very existence of all three Worlds. I called the Queen and informed her of what I think Gobrath is up to and she agrees with me, and so does Garrett."

George sat listening to her explain everything she found out and the plans made with both Worlds. He sent the heat away as she talked.

"My God, that idiot will destroy everything," George sank back in his chair.

"That's what the Queen and I think too." Then she was stunned by the look of incredible joy on his face. "George this is not good news." Her eyes widened in shock at his reaction.

"You heard the trees," he whispered. Pride for her filled him.

"Yes, but the rest of what I just told you is more important and deadly serious. You can be proud of me later for another of my gifts showing through. Right now we have a huge problem." She yelled at him.

The joy would not leave his eyes as he tried to douse the smile at her accomplishment. God she is beyond wonderful and she is my miracle, he thought.

"George we all have to be ready when Gobrath opens one of those portals." Stella tried to get him back on track.

"What do you want me to do?" He asked gently still marveling at her abilities.

"According to the trees we have to get the Coven to join us and I don't know how to convince them if Gertrude is unsuccessful."

"You need a Warlock to help convince them then." He nodded his head.

"The Elders are very set in their ways and may not want to help Gertrude and Tempest because they turned their backs on them, in their point of view."

"I could talk to Gertrude and find out what they said. If they refused her, then I can and will convince her to take me to them and I will get their assistance. No Coven of Witches would dare to go against a Warlock." He offered.

"We need them George, they must believe that."

"Rest assured my darling, they will do as I bid them." George's eyes narrowed. Witches have always been a bane to Warlocks but they would never risk their lives by refusing to carry out an order by one.

"For Gertrude's and Tempest's sake I hope you are not needed to convince them." Stella's heart went out to her friends.

"George, how fast can you get to me when the Queen informs us with the location of Gobrath?"

"A half a blink, no matter where I am at the time."

"Okay, that's good. Please contact me after you talk to Gertrude."

"I'll go to her now and get back to you as soon as I can."

After George left, Stella sat drumming her fingers on her desk. Almost everything and everyone was in place to attempt to stop Gobrath. All she could do now was to wait. And she was never good at that. Patience was never one of her virtues, not even when she worked on the Force.

"This is my time." Gobrath screamed out in his hiding place. "Once I open the way to all three Worlds I will trap my Father and show him that I am the only one to rule over all three Worlds. I will show him that I alone am the true ruler." Gobrath seethed. "That silly Fairy Queen will never be able to stop me once King

Gorkin is here and between the two of us we will first destroy her and her family and then I will destroy my father. I will rule over all the Worlds," Gobrath filled himself with self-righteousness. He could see all his dreams and ambitions coming true.

SEVENTEEN

L auren Wesley spent the rest of her day getting a spa treatment. She had her hair done and relaxed over a pedicure and manicure. By the end of it she was buffed and polished and felt wonderful.

When she returned home she went straight up to her home office and began researching for what was going to be her new hobby, murder for hire. With her husband out of the picture, she would at last have the time and financial means to give her full attention to it. Oh God, she hated to wait. This was something she knew she was born to do.

She began her research by looking up mercenary camps. The internet was a marvelous instrument for gaining every kind of information one could wish for.

You could find the makings and instructions for every bomb imaginable. You could find every kind of weapon needed for every use. Should you wish to use a poison, they too were there to find and all the effects they have. It was like looking at a how to instruction book. My God, every manner of deadly weapons can be found with instructions on building and using them. She began humming and singing out loud as she searched. She even thought of taking Martial Arts lessons.

Bentley noted down the time his Mistress left and returned to the home. He made a pretense of checking on the maids works upstairs and stealthily listened at her office door and heard her singing softly to herself.

Having some experience with computers, he wondered if he would get a chance to enter that room later and find out what she was looking into. It might only be her personal timetable and letters, but one never knew what else one might find. Some small part of him was actually starting to enjoy this cloak and dagger thing. And that did give him pause to wonder about this.

Following close behind this new found enjoyment came a sliver of conscience worming its way up making him wonder where his sense of duty and propriety had gone. What he is doing and about to do goes against all his training and years of service in the position he currently holds. Loyalty, confidentiality and complete respect to his employer should be his first priority.

Anticipation and execution of his duties to fulfill all his employer's wishes and needs are tantamount to his training and profession. A Butler worth his salt should always act with dignity and decorum and put the needs of his employer first. He comes from a long line of Butlers in his family. This has always been a staunch family tradition.

He shrugged all that off remembering his Master's life was in the balance of it all. Clamping firmly down on his conscience, he silently made his way back downstairs.

Bentley carried out his duties below while his Mistress was happily engaging in her own private activities. The household worked like clockwork, Bentley seen to that. The new cook was preparing the meals set out by the Mistress and the maids were busy with the duties of dusting, laundry and vacuuming. He checked to make sure all the flowers arranged in their vases throughout the house were fresh.

It was closing in on supper time when the cook was informed that the Mistress would not be here to take her meal. Lauren had called Bentley to the master bedroom. He found her in the process of packing suitcases. She instructed him that she was going to be away for a few days in the country.

No matter what questions sprang to his tongue, he kept quiet and only nodded to her.

"When would you like me to have the chauffeur bring the car around Madam?" He asked politely.

"Oh don't bother the chauffeur Bentley, I'll be driving myself. I'll be leaving in about a half hour."

"Very good Madam," Bentley bowed stiffly and left the room. He steeled his face to give nothing away as he made his way silently down the stairs. He went straight to his room closing the door behind him picked up his private phone and dialed Stella's number. Then returning it to its cradle after giving her a short report, he left his room to carry out his order to inform cook of the change of menu for the evening. Madam had instructed that cook prepare a light nutritious meal for the Master later when he returned home.

When the phone rang it was a welcome distraction. She listened to Bentley give a very short but detailed report. She heard a hint of stress in his voice as he spoke quietly to her.

"Bentley, you did the right thing telling me this. I believe that you may have just saved Mr. Wesley's life. When is he due home?"

"His plane should be arriving around seven o'clock tonight. He usually comes straight home, so he should be here an hour or an hour and a half after that depending on the baggage checks and traffic."

"Good, now I want you to call me when Mrs. Wesley has left and I may have further instructions for you."

"Very good Miss Blake." Bentley hung up the phone and took out his handkerchief to mop his sweaty brow. He felt a great sense of consolation not having a profession like Miss Blake. His nerves were beginning to fray and his mind quickly changed.

The short lived excitement he felt at all this spying and sneaking around swam away leaving him wishing never to have to do anything like this again. He wished only to go back to what he knows and enjoys, being a Butler. A safe and regimented orderly life was like a soft warm comfortable blanket. All he wanted now was to go back to that kind of life and never waiver from it ever again.

After this night is over he will be very happy to get back to doing the work he knows best and loves, being the best Butler he knows how to be. Never again did he ever wish to find himself in another situation like this one. He was not meant for a life of cloak and dagger. A shudder ran through him thinking of the unseemly and ugliness of such a profession that called for those attributes.

His personality and general makeup geared toward a loyal respectful and dignified profession. He liked a rigid structure to his life and wanted to get back to that as quickly as possible. Having a schedule and adhering to it is the way he wishes to live his life. He also wants his Master safe and to be able to serve him for many years to come. Mr. Wesley has proven to be a most considerate and generous of employers. From now on he will do all that is in his power to see to his Master's wishes and comfort.

Stella called George on his cell phone and gave him the good news. She could visualize the smile on his face as he thanked her. She knew who the target was now and George and his team would catch the person and that case will soon come to an end.

"The butler has just made my day. The team will be climbing all over themselves to get a crack at interviewing the woman when we get her in." He had been in a very heated argument with Gertrude when Stella called. The news she gave him lifted his spirits.

"Stella, when Bentley calls again to let you know his Master has returned home, find out when he retires for the night and have him let my people in then. I'll wait for your call." He said and hung up and turned his attention back to Gertrude again.

"Gertrude this is no time for our differences to get in the way of helping each other. If Gobrath succeeds there will be no one left to differ with. Now," his voice boomed out. "You will take me to the Coven and I will speak to the Elders whether they wish it or not." He commanded.

Gertrude knew she had no choice now. She was ordered by a Warlock to do his bidding and could not refuse. It was one of the most absolute laws for Witches. With a heavy heart she reached out to take her daughter's hand and then held the other out for George to take. Witches were ingrained to always do as a Warlock commanded them. Even the Elders have to obey a Warlock.

In a blink they were standing in the middle of a little community. Sensing a Warlock in their presence, within seconds all doors flew open and the community of Witches came running out with wands raised.

George instantly formed a shield around the three of them and stood glowering at the crowd. He watched the crowd separate giving way so three elderly women could hobble forward. 'They must be the Elders,' he thought.

"How dare you come into the sanctity of our Coven Warlock!" one of the elderly women screamed at him. "Leave us now." She lifted her wand in a feeble attempt.

"Lower you wands Witches," His voice boomed out. "I George, descendant of Prince Gareg of the Warlock World command you." Fireballs grew in his hands as he glared at the crowd of Witches.

All arms wielding a wand instantly lowered. They were unable to disobey a direct order from a Warlock.

Fear grew in every pair of eyes now that they were rendered helpless before him. Even the three elderly Witches were forced to lower their wands.

"You have betrayed us Gertrude," one of the elderly Witches spat. "There is nowhere you can hide from us. We will seek you out and destroy you for this," she threatened.

"You will not harm Gertrude or her daughter," George barked at her. "They came to you for help. They told you of the danger we all face and you denied her. For that you will pay, but that will come after this danger is dealt with." He threatened the three.

He had to give the Elders credit. He just issued out a direct threat to them and they stood firm, not flinching an inch. These were very determined minded Elders.

"You all know of the spirits of the trees and they told my wife that the Coven is needed if we are to have any chance of winning this battle. I order this Coven to give its aid to us.

"Much is to be done and the time is short. My wife will seek out the spirits of the trees again to find out what your part must be and you will obey. If the three Elders had chosen to help instead of seeking revenge on its own kind I would not have had to come here and order you to do so."

George noticed the crowd's reaction to his words. Most of them gave a slight nod while only a few older one's stood glowering at him in defiance, sticking to the ruling of the Elders.

He was seeing the beginnings of a revolt in the Coven and it hurt him. He knew what a Coven meant to Witches. They needed the Coven like humans needed air to live. They could never find peace or happiness without it. They cannot survive without their Coven. Gertrude and Tempest were proof of that.

But what was before them all had him steel his heart to their future pains in order to force them to do their part.

"We will obey only because you left us no other choice. We must obey a direct order from Warlocks. If you are truly here for this reason only, then I suggest you put away your fireballs." Yet another of the Elders addressed him.

The request stunned him for a moment. He had not realized that he still held the fireballs in his hand. He quickly extinguished them nodded and turned to Gertrude.

"I must leave now. If you wish to go back I can take you with me." His eyes softened when he looked at her pained face.

"I will take Tempest home myself. We will await your call when we are needed." She gave one more sorrowful glance back to her Coven then took her daughter's hand and vanished.

George turned to the Elders, "You have done your Coven a huge disservice by not adapting to the changing times." He glared at them when he saw the fierce defiance on the old women's faces.

"You have our existence in your hands," one of the Elders dared to speak. "We have lived our lives and survived because of our rulings and laws. We know you can destroy us, but we will not go without a fight Warlock."

"What you have done Witch is to keep this Coven in the dark ages. What is coming our way will need the help of this Coven along with the help of the Fairly Blood and Warlock Blood. Heed my warning that you do as I command." George spat back at her.

George transported himself back to his car and drove to the precinct. He had to alert the team that there could be a possible hit planned for tonight. This time he could tell them the tip came from the Butler of the intended victim.

He just hoped and prayed that Gobrath would not open a portal when his men were in the middle of stopping a murder.

Once again the squad felt that Stella interfered in their work. Had she mentioned the Butler's role in this case and the fact she kept that information from them, had Sally steaming. It seems that all the information they've been given is coming from her. The fact they were told by the Lt. to watch Mrs. Wesley at the funeral told them that their boss got that from Stella. This is a solid case of interference in Police business. If she'd have handed over all the information in the beginning she gathered including getting a Butler to help her, they would've been the ones to act first by getting warrants and extra funding for stakeouts.

Sally couldn't help steaming over this slap in the face by their old Lieutenant. Stella was the best when she worked for the Force, but the fact remains that she no longer works for it now. It not only hurt but was very disrespectful to this squad and to this House. Sally found that she can't get over the hurt she feels over this.

EIGHTEEN

All day, Stella was poised for a message from her Queen. Her nerves were strung out. When the phone rang she jumped.

"Stella Blake, Private Investigator," she blurted out.

"Miss Blake, Master Wesley has returned and is upstairs unpacking." Bentley whispered into the phone.

"Very good Bentley. I need you to do one more thing for me and I promise that this will end tonight." She made her voice sound convincing.

"I don't know how much more I can take of this Miss Blake," he paused. "Tell me what you wish me to do." He tried to sound brave.

"Call me the moment Mr. Wesley retires for the night and then I need you to keep a look out outside and silently let in the police that will be outside the door. Lock the door after you let them in and reset the alarm. Then you should go to your quarters and wait. Can you do this?"

"Yes, I can do that. I will call you when he retires for the night. But please I beg of you, let this end tonight and keep Mr. Wesley safe. If you cannot end this tonight I don't think my nerves will take anymore." His stiff reserve was draining out.

"Bentley you have been a great help in ending this and if I'm right, it will all be over with tonight. Thank you for your help and I'm sure that Betty will thank you when this is over too."

Just thinking of the cook had some of his resolve return. He realized now how terrified she has been and why and he wanted her back here feeling safe and doing the job she loves. He has a deep friendship for Mrs. Vanhorn and only wants her safe.

"I cannot imagine how Mrs. Vanhorn has suffered the terror she has been forced to live with. I will do as you ask for both my Master and the cook. For their sakes I hope this does end tonight."

Stella noticed that Bentley sounded stronger because of the two people he cherished.

Stella called George to let him know he could alert his people to go into the house tonight as soon as she got the call from Bentley.

Everything was set up. They were all waiting on the call to put their plan into action.

Bertrum was disappointed when he arrived home to find that his wife had left for a few days retreat. After finishing up some paperwork in his home office he went down to dine alone. Tired from his flight and being alone, he decided to retire early. He called his wife in the country and after a short conversation headed upstairs to the master bedroom to get a good night's sleep. As soon as he felt it safe, Bentley peered through the window and saw the police waiting outside the door. He opened it and let them in. They split up, some concealing themselves downstairs and the others upstairs.

He called Stella to let her know that her instructions were carried out.

Stella called George to tell him what the Butler told her.

It was all set up. The police were in the house and Bentley in his private quarters pacing back and forth. All they could do now was to wait. The house was dark giving the appearance that everyone had retired for the evening.

Around midnight, a car crawled up the laneway with the headlights out. It parked in front of the house and a figure in all black climbed out. After glancing around, the figure headed straight for the door. Nervous, it took the person a few minutes to unlock the door and then to turn off the alarm.

Once that was done, the figure leaned against the door and took a deep breath. Unknown to her, she was being watched by a cop from the room off the foyer.

The figure slowly quietly turned left and started up the stairs. Reaching the top, she made her way down the hall to the master bedroom. She stopped and listened at the door and heard the sounds of Bertrum snoring. Taking a deep breath, she opened the door and walked in.

When she stood beside the bed, she raised a large knife and began to plunge it down and found her arm seized in a firm grip preventing her from plunging the knife into the man's heart. She let out a scream.

Everything happened at once. The lights went on and Bertrum sprang up at the sound in a sitting position. The woman dressed all in black kept screaming and then collapsed.

Finding his bedroom full of people had Bertrum confused at first and then barking out questions.

"Who the hell are you? What are you all doing here? How did you get in? What the hell is going on here?" His confused state from waking from a dead sleep had him miss the fact that a woman all dressed in black was being held by a couple of men. A man holding a large carving knife that gleamed under the lights caught his eye.

"Mr. Wesley, do you recognize this person?" One of the undercover cops asked holding the woman. He whipped off her balaclava revealing her face.

Bertrum blinked his eyes and then stared at the woman. "Of course I know her. She is Barbara Danvers. She is the wife of Kenneth Danvers of Danvers Industries and a good friend of my wife's."

"Thank you sir," the cop smiled.

"Barbara what the hell is going on and why are you here dressed like that and in my bedroom. I don't understand any of this." He shook his head to try and clear it.

"Who are you people?" Still confused, it wasn't sinking in yet.

"We are the police and this woman came here to kill you tonight." One of the cops stated.

"Oh that's just nonsense. Tell them Barbara that it's nonsense." Then something struck him. "Who let you all in? Bentley," he yelled out.

Bentley was standing outside his door. He heard the scream and rushed up the stairs but could not force himself to enter at that time. He came in now that his Master had called for him.

"Sir," he said, his face ghastly white.

"Bentley did you let all these people into the house tonight?"

"Yes sir," he gulped. "It was necessary sir in order to save your life."

"Save my life, what do you mean save my life?" he demanded.

"If Bentley had not cooperated with us Mr. Wesley you would have been murdered tonight." Another cop, the one holding the knife volunteered.

"Oh that is utter rubbish. Why would anyone want to murder me? Barbara is a friend of ours." He tossed the explanation aside.

"Sir, Barbara Danvers came here tonight to murder you and I'm sorry to inform you that your wife is in on it." The same cop stated. "She gave this woman the key and codes to your house for that specific reason. We took this knife from her." he held it up.

Bertrum's head snapped up. What this officer was telling him could not be true. He would not believe it. He loves his wife and knows that she loves him. There is no reason for his wife to want him harmed. This simply could not be true.

Then his eyes took in the way their friend was dressed and the big knife one of the cops was holding. His brain just could not bring itself to believe what his eyes were telling him.

"Why," he asked her, it was the only question that came to him.

"The reason behind this will be clear once we get Mrs. Danvers into interrogation." The cop holding her said.

Barbara fainted again.

As he predicted, the squad was biting at the bit to get the chance to do the interrogating. It was good to see their spirits so high. He turned to them and assigned two of them to go in and begin the proceedings while the others waited in the observation room.

Barbara Danvers was slumped in her chair, her one hand handcuffed to the table when Tom and Sally walked in. Her eyes held a blank look as she looked up when the door opened.

'This was not real. None of this could be happening,' she kept saying it over and over again in her head. She only lifted her head when she heard her name. Her eyes stared blankly at Sally Pride.

"Hello," she spoke softly trying to remember if she knew this woman sitting across from her. "Do we know each other?" She asked confused. Even being handcuffed to the table didn't register with her at the moment.

"No we don't Mrs. Danvers, but we are going to get to know each other very well." Sally stared back at her.

"Oh," was all Barbara could think to say.

"What were you doing at the Wesley's house tonight?" Tom spoke sharply causing Barbara to snap her head around to look at him. Then she looked around at her surroundings.

"But I'm not at the Wesley house." Her brow creased. "I'm afraid I don't know where I am."

"You, Mrs. Danvers are in the police station in an interrogation room," Tom piped up again. "Now answer the question. What were you doing at the Wesley's house tonight?"

The police station. How did I get here? Did I make a mistake? Barbara's brow creased trying hard to remember but her mind refused to take her where she wanted it to go. Her eyes full of confusion she kept staring at the man across from her.

Sally saw that Barbara was in full shock. She knew Tom's hammering at her would only make her sink further into herself and they could lose her mentally. She reached over and touched his hand. When he turned to her all she did was shake her head. Being a cop for years and with this team, he picked up on her silent meaning and leaned back in his chair to let her take over for now.

"Mrs. Danvers," Sally spoke gently. When she got Barbara to look in her direction she continued. "Can you tell me what you did today?" Figuring if she took her back to the beginning of the day, she might come out of her shock.

Barbara watched Sally's face and saw a kindness in her eyes. She warmed to this and began detailing her day for her. She had such a lovely day, planning out the schedules for her house staff. She remembered the day flying by as she did the things she loved doing, organizing her home, puttering in the garden and getting ready for her weekly lunch date. . .

As soon as she mentioned the lunch date, fear filled her eyes.

"Go on," Sally prompted her. "You went to your luncheon. Who did you take this luncheon with Mrs. Danvers?"

"Oh just some friends," Barbara did not want to give out the names.

Sally opened a file in front of her and rifled through some pages until she came across the one she wanted. "Let me see if I can help you with that." Sally rattled off the names of all the women that were at the luncheon and watched the surprised expression on Barbara's face. "Is that correct Mrs. Danvers?"

"Uh, yes," Barbara couldn't understand how this woman knew the names of everyone at her table in Chez Francois.

"Good, that's very good Mrs. Danvers." Sally smiled and paused. "Now can you explain to me and my partner here how you came to have the code and keys to the Wesley home? We found them in your pocket."

Should she tell them Lauren gave them to her? What excuse should she give for Lauren to have given them to her? Maybe she should ask Lauren what she should do. "I'd like to make a phone call please."

"You have been read your rights and you waived Counsel Mrs. Danvers." Tom leaned forward.

"Oh but I don't want to call a lawyer, I need to speak with Lauren." She stated innocently.

"Are you telling us that Mrs. Wesley gave you a key and the code to her house?" Tom jumped on the information.

"Yes, I mean no, I mean I need to talk to her first." Barbara said frantically.

"I'm sorry Mrs. Danvers, but you cannot call her at this time, maybe later after we finish here." Sally lied keeping her voice calm and gentle.

"Oh, alright, yes, thank you." She felt calmer talking to the woman.

"You're welcome. Now since we found you inside the house and you say Mrs. Wesley gave you the key and code, tell us why you were there tonight." Sally urged her on.

Another lie.

"Well it's the plan you see and Lauren wanted to change the order so I had to do my part ahead of schedule."

"So you were supposed to help out Mrs. Wesley." Sally didn't want to say the words kill or murder fearing she would close down on them.

"Well, yes. You see we all drew names and I drew Lauren's. But it wasn't her turn, you see. She changed the order because she didn't want to wait for her peace and to have her life stay the same. We all want that. None of us wanted to ever go back to the way we lived before we married. It's very simple you see."

"We are beginning to see. Can you explain this plan to us?"

Completely forgetting where she was, Barbara smiled and outlined the plan, explaining the simplicity of it. Telling them how it was entirely the husbands fault for not wanting them anymore after they all tried so hard to please them. How none of them wanted to go back to the lives they had before marrying their husbands.

"So you see if they had only kept their vows and were faithful none of this would be necessary. Lauren said we were only protecting ourselves."

"Are you saying that Lauren Wesley came up with this plan? And you all agreed to it?" Tom frowned at her.

"I'm sure being a man you wouldn't understand," Barbara shook her head at Tom. "You can see that it was necessary can't you?" She looked at Sally for understanding.

Instead of answering, Sally pushed a clear evidence bag towards Barbara containing the knife she held over Mr. Wesley in his bedroom.

Barbara looked down at it and paled. She could still feel it in her hands and the nausea she felt wielding it over Bertrum's heart came back hitting her hard. She threw up all over the table before slumping back in her chair in a dead faint.

"Picked the wrong woman for that job," Tom sneered.

"Yeah, I think we got the weakest link in this group of murderers." Sally frowned.

George watched as the medical aide came in and dealt with Mrs. Danvers. He didn't need to see any more. They had enough with her testimony and the testimony of Mr. Wesley to pick up the leader of the pack. It was just a matter of getting all the sworn statements and evidence logged in and the warrants issued to put this case to bed. It was going to be a slam dunk case for the Crown.

NINETEEN

The rest of the week went by without incident. All the women in the pact of murder were picked up and questioned before booking. Each member of his squad had a chance to interrogate members of this unusual group of greedy angry women. George wanted the pleasure of questioning Lauren himself.

Lauren's face was livid with rage at her co-conspirators. 'How dare they spill everything, the cowards', she thought. She centered her rage on Barbara for being so stupid as to get caught. It had to be her fault. The plan was perfect so she had to have made a monstrous mistake. It was so simple. All she had to do was get in go up and plunge the knife into her husband, walk out, lock up and go home. It worked three times in a row; even she made it through without incident. It had to be Barbara's fault.

Even though all her cohorts turned on her, she had to find a way out of this mess. She did not deserve to go to jail, not now that she just found her true calling.

"Well now Mrs. Wesley, according to your friends, you have all been very busy scheming, planning and carrying out a murderous hobby. And according to them you are the one that came up with the idea and the plans for carrying it out."

"That's just ridiculous. I don't know why they would say that about me. I'm shocked to find out that some of them committed murder." Lauren sat rigid in her chair giving the air of shock and outrage.

"Oh come now, Mrs. Wesley, they all named you as the ring leader. Why don't you just tell me your side of the story?" George produced a bag holding a large carving knife. He saw the moment she recognized it as her own from her set of pearl handled kitchen knives.

"Where did you get that from?" She demanded.

"We took this from your friend and it matches the set in your home when we searched it. Do you recognize this knife?" George cocked his head.

"Well of course I do," she sneered. "That's from the set my husband bought for our cook for a Christmas gift. Why do you have it?" Thinking fast she figured she could blame the cook.

"This knife was used to kill Mr. Foxworth. Forensic found blood on it and matched that blood to Johnathan Foxworth."

"The cook killed Johnathan? But why?" She snatched at the glimmer of hope.

"No, Mrs. Wesley, your cook did not kill Mr. Foxworth. You did with this knife. We also found your fingerprints on the handle." She forgot that she took the knife before dressing. She wasn't wearing her gloves at that time.

"Well of course my finger prints would be on it. After all, the set is inside my home. My fingerprints are all over my home." The glimmer was dimming just a bit.

"According to your cook, you have never entered the kitchen. Bentley, your Butler gives her your orders. We have her statement. And it might interest you to know that we also have a statement from her about a conversation she overheard between yourself and Brianna, one of your luncheon friends, who as it happens is being charged with murder. We have her statement as well."

That glimmer of hope just blew out like a birthday candle. Panic set in now. "I want my lawyer," Lauren shouted.

"You can have a bevy of lawyers but they won't do you any good. Mrs. Lauren Wesley, you are charged with the murder of Johnathan Foxworth and six counts of conspiracy to commit murder." He got up opened the door to let the officers in. They pulled her up, slapped handcuffs on her and led her away to booking. Lauren was too shocked at this point to put up any fight at all. She still felt that her plan was foolproof and that she will be released soon. She went with the officer to take her down to booking. All the while she went through the motions she felt that she will get off this charge and then she planned to come at the police and the silly women with a vengeance.

It was amazing how all the men left on the list were more than happy to see their wives charged and in a cell, well, all but Bertrum. He was still shocked by his wife's part in all of it. He could not understand how she did not know how much he truly loved her. It was like he was morning her death instead of rejoicing in his living.

Stella could not begin another case until the problem of the portals had been dealt with. George closed his case and his squad was still reeling with exhilaration over it. Deb's shower was planned for tomorrow night and Stella hoped fervently that it would go off without a hitch. And Betty Vanhorn was once again in the Wesley employ happily cooking for the household with Bentley hovering over her like a mother hen. She found that she was being treated with more compassion and respect by the Master of the house. This went a long way to help her to deal with the danger, terror and turmoil she just went through. To show her gratitude she put all her culinary training to good use in providing the best meals for Mr. Wesley. She knew all his favourite dishes and made sure that she prepared them perfectly for him, keeping in mind his health issues. Betty hoped that her meals will not only comply with Doctor's orders but be delicious enough to take his mind off his heartbreak as well.

Garrett decided it was time to go back to the woods and find out what they could learn from the trees. The Coven was ready to do its part once they knew what it was and under orders from the Warlock George to do their part.

He called Stella to meet him in the clearing. It was getting easier and easier for Stella to transport. They stood a small distance from each other as they brought the heat into themselves for the transformation.

Once they were transformed they looked like two huge Greek gods towering higher than the tallest tree bordering the clearing. Stella floated larger than life, her flaming red hair whipping around her face, her body dressed in a flowing white gown with diamond straps criss-crossing her bodice and a glowing jeweled crown adorning her head. Garrett's long shining raven hair blew in the wind caused by them and he too was dressed in a white toga affair but without a crown on his head. Their eyes shot out sparks.

Garrett called to the trees to speak to them both. Within seconds they heard the rush of many hushed voices. Garrett pointed to one tree indicating to Stella to open her mind to that one. They both concentrated to bring only that voice to their minds.

The other trees fell silent so the chosen one could speak alone.

"You told us of the black. You told us that the Coven is needed. We need you now to tell us what the Coven must do." Stella's voice boomed out around them.

The tree Garrett indicated bowed its tip to touch the ground and then lift up again. The other trees of the woods remained silent giving way to the one the two chose to speak to them.

After listening to the tree, they found that time, space and dimension had no affect on plant life. They were as one no matter the place or time. It appeared that they were in communication with the vegetation of the Fairy and Warlock worlds.

The chosen tree explained in detail the role the Coven must play. Even with this special communication between worlds, the trees could not give the specific location of which portal would be used. However, they have made a pact with the animals of the woods that should it be in the clearing, one would be dispatched immediately to alert her. But regardless of the location, the Coven will be needed to perform their part.

Garrett and Stella thanked the woods for their help and slowly released the heat. They floated down to the ground. For the first time since Stella transformed, she did not pool on the ground from the drain on her energy but felt exhilarated. Garrett beamed with pride at his daughter's growth in her gifts.

"I'll tell George what they said and he will tell the Coven." She said to her father.

"Would you like me to transport you back to the Manor?" Garrett still smiled.

"If you don't mind, how about I try to transport us there?" She was feeling so pleased with herself.

"Then take my hand and let's go." Garrett laughed.

Taking hold of his hand, Stella took a deep breath and gave it her all. She had them standing in the front yard in a blink. She couldn't help doing a little jump for joy at her success.

Garrett picked her up and twirled her around in pure joy at his daughter's accomplishment. She giggled with sheer delight. After he set her down they walked hand in hand into the Manor.

From inside, Stella called George and told him what the trees told her. She was still riding a high when her mother came into the room to see the joy on her daughter's face.

Garrett went straight to her and told her everything that happened.

"Oh you should have seen her Wanda. Our girl is really coming in to her true self. I am so proud of her." He hugged Wanda. "She still needs more training but she is learning so fast. I can't be more proud of her."

Wanda beamed with pride over her daughter's growth and success. Her eyes filled with joyful tears. "Oh my darling daughter, to think of the years you spent denying what you are and now to see how you have embraced it, you have made me so happy." She turned her face and wept on Garrett's shirt.

"I'm so sorry I was so stubborn for those years mother. I guess I was just afraid to admit to being different from everyone else." She walked over to put her hand on her mother's shoulder.

Wanda leapt from Garrett's embrace to wrap her arms around her daughter. "You have made me so proud and so happy my darling."

The two women stood embracing each other and weeping on each other. Stella wept for the peace she finally found in herself and the joy she brought to her mother. But in the back of her mind there was still the niggling feeling of the way she betrayed her family when they first came into contact with her father. That simply would not go away for her.

Maria walked in to find everyone mopping away tears. She had no idea they were tears of joy. She reached into her apron and drew out her wand waving it high glancing around for danger.

Garrett gently touched her arm and shook his head at her to show her there was no need for concern. She looked up at him confused but kept a firm grip on the wand just in case.

"What is it?" Maria asked.

Hearing Maria's voice, Wanda turned to her. "Oh Maria it is the best thing that could ever happen. Stella is truly one with herself now and embracing it." She began to weep again.

Of course Maria was happy for her friend, but at the moment her concern over Gertrude and Tempest kept her from jumping for joy. Her heart was breaking for the friend she knew as a girl. The Coven would surely hunt them down once this battle was over, if they won the battle. They have the power to call Gertrude and Tempest to them should they wish to go that route. There was no escaping the Elders.

Some of her concern was noticed by Garrett and he laid a gentle hand on her shoulder again in comfort to let her know he knew how she was feeling.

"I'm sure it will all work out once everything settles down." He whispered to her offering his sympathy for her plight.

"We can only hope the Goddess is willing to shine on us." She whispered back acknowledging his kind words to her. All Witches put their faith in the Goddess of the Elements. They have many ceremonies held at different times of the year to offer their worship, belief, faith and praise to this Goddess of Nature. This belief is woven into their very fiber and is held most high to all Witches. She is as real to them as God is to all others in the World.

Gertrude and her daughter Tempest were in such pain not being allowed back inside their Coven. It broke Maria's heart to know that her best friend and daughter were outcasts and had no support. At least, she had Wanda in her life to make up for not having the Coven. Gertrude and her daughter didn't even have a friend like that to comfort them. God they must be feeling so alone and frightened by now. To have no one, not even the Coven to rely on must be so painful for her dear friend. To a Witch, the Coven is their life. She gave that up to save and stay with what the Coven deemed as their enemy. But her friend Gertrude didn't even have that in her life now. Maria's eyes teared up at that painful thought. She knew for Gertrude living outside the Coven was like living in a void, like not living at all. She has no direction or sense of safety in her life now. It must be like she is floating on the sea of uncertainty. Maria knew that if things didn't change for her she would surely die or give up on living which meant the same thing in her mind. This is a pain like no other and her heart broke for her childhood friend.

Stella left the Manor to drive back to her office.

Without knowing which portal and where it was, she found herself pacing back and forth across the room. She felt odd and unsettled having nothing to do. This was a first for her.

Just as she was making her tenth pass across the room, the door opened and Louise came in.

"I thought I'd drop by and let you know that everything is ready for the shower tomorrow night." She glided past her and took a seat. Once she was settled she turned to Stella, still standing in the middle of the room. "I also wanted to know what you got Deb for a shower gift." She smiled.

'Shower, tomorrow, gift,' Stella's mind went into panic mode.

"You did get her something didn't you?" Now Louise's eyes narrowed. The look on Stella's face was enough to tell her that she had forgotten all about the event and getting a gift for her friend.

"I, well," she hesitated. "I've been a little busy Louise." Stella's face went crimson.

"Stella Colleen Blake Smale, do not stand there and tell me that you forgot to get something special for your dearest and closest friend." Louise snapped out, her face fuming.

The sheer disregard for her friend's feelings had her gearing up for a full blown-out rage. Louise jumped out of her chair and stood with fisted hands on her hips ready to tear a strip off this tall lean uncaring redhead.

"I can understand your job keeping you from helping with the planning and helping with the details and decorating, but I will not listen to one excuse from you to show up empty handed. This is your closest and dearest friend. I will not allow you to break that dear girl's heart." Louise's voice raised two octaves.

The heat from Louise's anger hit Stella full in the face like a fist. Her head snapped up and her green eyes narrowed. Just behind them sparks began to build. Her natural reflexes were to meet anger with anger and she could feel the heat begin to build in her. If it was anyone else, she knew she could rein in the temper. But Louise always seemed to manage to get behind her resolve and she was ready to battle.

Forgetting herself Stella raised her arms and was on the brink of letting the heat take over when she heard a voice behind her. Suddenly her arms were held in a tight grip preventing her from transforming right there and then.

"Louise," She heard George's voice behind her. "Did you come here to fight with my wife?" He tightened his grip when Stella began to struggle to be free.

"Of course not." Louise fumed. "I just found out that Stella was," she put up two fingers of each hand and made the quotation sign with them, "too busy to buy her dear friend a shower gift."

"Well as it turns out you are very mistaken. We do have a gift for the lucky couple. A pair of tickets to the Bahamas for their honeymoon," he raised an eyebrow at his foster sister.

"Oh, nice save brother," Louise sneered at him. "I bet this is the first time Stella even heard about it."

"I was going to surprise her tonight with the news. But thanks to you that surprise is spoiled." George let go of Stella's wrists and put an arm around her to lead her over to take her seat behind her desk.

Stella was still recovering from almost making the biggest mistake of her life. Sparks were still flickering behind her eyes. She knew she had to calm down and get herself under control. 'What was it about Louise that she could make her forget to keep her secret hidden and lash out at her?' she wondered.

Stella jumped out of her seat and ran out of the room up the stairs to her private quarters. She needed to put space between her and Louise.

If George hadn't shown up when he did she would have revealed herself to his sister. Yes they were two strong women but she had to find some way of not letting this feisty woman to get under her skin and get the better of her from now on.

A smile played on her face when she thought about the look on her face if ever she did find out.

George watched her go and turned to his sister.

"Louise, why don't you sit down and I'll get us all a cup of coffee." George offered smiling at his sister. "I'll just go up and see if Stella is alright." He left her to go to Stella.

He found her pacing in her kitchen.

"Darling, I'm sorry I interfered, but I don't think you really want Louise to see what we are." He said softly.

"God George, she just keeps pushing the wrong buttons where it concerns me." She rubbed her hands over her face.

"I agree that she is a force to be reckoned with but I can't help loving her," George smiled. If you think you have your temper under control, we should go back before she decides to come looking for us." George recommended.

Stella agreed and joined him in going back to her office. What he said made sense and she knew that Louise is a Human. She just wished that she can control her anger better where Louise is concerned. What the Hell is so different about Louise that she can't seem to just shake off her interfering and annoying barbs?

Louise looked from one to the other as they walked back into the office again. But lately she sensed something was very strange going on with the two of them and she hated being left out of the loop. She relaxed her hands and took her seat again. One day, she vowed, she would get to the bottom of this. But right now she felt her first instincts about Stella were confirmed. She is not the genteel sophisticated woman that should be chosen to married her foster brother. Stella could never fulfill the role of a good hostess and Chatelaine for that Palatial home of his.

Now that they were all settled sitting around the desk with a cup of coffee, the tension between them faded. Louise's anger was gone. It was in her nature not to hold on to anger. Once she spewed she was over it. But looking at Stella, she realized that she was still a little miffed and concerned for her foster brother.

Stella still remembered the generosity of Louise for not charging Debra for stealing her necklace at one of her friend's functions. At that time she showed the generosity of her nature and had Stella liking her for that at that time. But what she didn't like was the way Louise always felt righteous in not calling first before showing up on a person's doorstep. She did wonder where that trait came from.

"That's a wonderful gift and I'm sure the two of them will appreciate it very much." She smiled up at her brother. "I also came over to find out what Stella will be wearing. Since she is scheduled to walk down the runway, we need to be able to describe it like it was a real fashion show." She looked over at Stella.

Stella looked blank for a moment. Then she recalled some conversation about the mock fashion show. She hadn't had time to think about the shower at all with everything going on, let alone what she was going to wear for it.

"I believe Stella mentioning something about her strapless green sequence gown. Is that right dear?" He cast his glance to his wife with just a hint of smirk showing at the corners of his mouth.

She frowned at him knowing very well that she never mentioned anything about what she was going to wear. Then she smiled over at Louise.

"Yes, that's right, the Versace gown."

"Oh it really is too bad that you won't wear one of Deb's creations but you do wear Dior and Versace very well." Louise conceded. "Good, I'll let Angela know. She will be narrating the fashion show." Louise couldn't help but wonder how Stella could afford to buy creations made by very high-end designers. She didn't think that cops or P.I.'s were paid that much to afford those prices. She hoped that Stella didn't have George purchase those expensive items for her.

"I wore the wedding dress she made for me." Stella offered in her defense.

"And you looked absolutely beautiful in it. Deb is the most fantastic designer." Louise beamed.

"She's the best in my books." Stella agreed. She was so proud of her friend. Her eyes filled with pride for Deb. "As far as I know there is no other designer that can come close to her."

Now that the tempers were banked they sat around chatting about the shower and touched on the relationship building between Dave Palmer and Louise. Louise's eyes lit up whenever she talked about the love of her life. Stella could see that her foster sister-in-law and her friend were a good solid match so far. But there was a niggling doubt in the back of her mind and she didn't know where that stemmed from. That sudden doubt had her very worried for her friend David Palmer. The only thing she wanted is that Dave will not be hurt in this relationship. She didn't make friends easily but when she did she would try to protect them in any way possible.

Louise left them feeling better and excited about the event they were all attending the next evening.

Stella turned to George, "God she has a real knack for knowing what buttons to push and I can't seem to stop reacting to them."

A bit of devilment came into his eyes as he reached over to take her hand. "May I suggest then that you turn your mind to fluffy pink bunnies when she pushes those sensitive buttons?" He couldn't help the laugh that bubbled up and spewed out.

"Pink bunnies, hmm," she narrowed her eyes at him. "Oh yeah, I'll get right on that one." But then the vision of pink bunnies popped into her head and she too had to laugh. But deep down she felt there was something off and she didn't want to worry him about this feeling she has. For some strange reason she kept thinking that Louise has an agenda against her and wondered what that can be.

"George she really does have to work on calling first before popping in." Stella frowned.

George knew she was right and couldn't understand the bad manners his foster sister was displaying. "Stella, she was not raise to show such bad manners and yes, I too think she should show better manners than she has recently." He frowned.

This had him thinking too that something was off with his foster-sister. As much as he didn't want to think anything badly about her since he loves her so much, he just couldn't get rid of the feeling that something was not adding up when it came to her behavior lately.

George could not stop the feelings that Stella's words instilled in him. He owed everything to his foster parents. They took him in when his parents deserted him. His loyalty to them was paramount. He'd always stood up for and protected Louise, but now because of what Stella said, he began having his first doubts about her.

This was very difficult for him and he knew he has to think about what Stella suggested to him.

Stella noticed the change in George straight away. Now she was sorry for placing any doubts about his foster sister in his mind. She knows the depth of love he carries for her and her parents for taking him in and raising him as their own. Stella wondered if that was the first time he ever felt love since his real parents deserted him.

TWENTY

The ballroom at the Belvedere was crowded by the time George and Stella arrived the next evening. Although George made sure he got Stella there before Deb and Richard were due to arrive.

People were darting everywhere laughing and talking. Mr. and Mrs. Styles were ushering people who were not participating in the fashion show to their seats, while Louise tried rounding up the participants of the runway walkers. Angela stood at the podium arranging the cue cards she would use to announce and describe the outfits the amateur models will be wearing. She handed a copy of the order to Louise in order to organize the women to step out in the correct order.

It was a beehive of activity.

Stella checked her watch and saw they only had about a half hour before the guests of honour were due to make their entrance. She took a quick glance around. Louise grabbed her arm and began pulling her to the curtained off area.

Angela had done a marvelous job on the decorations. It looked exactly like a real fashion show. Rows of chairs now being filled were placed on both sides of the raised runway. What would have been a dressing area was cordoned off with a red curtain at the back of the runway.

The runway itself was draped in red velvet to match the curtains. Lights were hung high overhead attached to booms to follow the would-be models as they walked. A canvas of rainbow coloured curtains billowed above the runway. It was truly amazing.

They could hear the cheers on the other side of the curtain. Deb and Richard must have arrived. Louise got busy lining up all the women in the right order and they waited for Angela to give the signal to start the fashion parade.

This will be the first time Debra sat in the audience and not busy behind the curtain getting all the models ready for a showing.

They listened to the cheers and laughter. It took a long time for the room to settle down. Angela popped her head in from behind the curtain and whispered for everyone to get ready. Her eyes glowed. She was so excited, one might think this was all for her benefit. She was absolutely thrilled to do this for Deb's sake.

One by one they paraded down the runway at Louise's signal. Some walked like a wedding march, some stomped the way they thought real models would do, and some simply walking normal and smiled and waved at the crowd seated on both sides.

The entire room filled with the sounds of laughter and oohing and awing and loud clapping as each woman in turn took to the runway. Deb's delighted squeals could be heard over it all. When Stella walked out, she saw the tears running down her friend's beaming face. Her own eyes welled seeing how thrilled and delighted Deb was.

Deb came back behind the curtain when the last of her friends finished up. She jumped at Stella and clung to her like a skin diver's suit, laughing and crying with pure joy.

"It was so amazing," she sobbed. "Louise told me you thought of the theme. Oh Stella, it was the most absolute best gift ever. I love you so much for thinking of this for me." Then she pulled back to look up at her friend. "Richard was just blown away with it too."

"Hey there, watch the waterworks or I'm going to need rubber boots," Stella laughed down at her little pixie friend. "I'm glad you like it, but really it was all

Angela, Louise and my family. I'm sorry I didn't have any time to help out with it."

Guilt filled her for not being there for her friend. It pained her to know that Deb would drop everything for her and she couldn't do the same.

"You thought of this fashion show Stella, that's a real biggy in my books. So what's next on the agenda?" Deb looked around at the room still filled with the women that took place in the fashion show.

"I have no idea, but knowing Angela and Louise like we do, they must have something very special planned for you. Let's go out and find out what it is." She draped her arm around Deb and walked them through to the room full of people.

It was special. By the time they entered the room, it was transformed to look like a huge working studio for Deb. Gone was the raised platform. Tables were set around for the guests. Each table was draped with a tablecloth with prints of Deb's other fashion designs on them.

The walls were lined with designer work tables with all kinds of materials flowing over them. The center pieces for the guests' tables were fat coloured mason jars filled with pencils, slivers of charcoal, scissors and measuring tapes. Each end of the room held a mannequin half covered like a project in the making. It was a designer's dream come true for a wedding shower.

Stella led her over to the table set up for the guests of honour. She was cooing and weeping all the way. George, Richard, Louise and Dave were already seated and enjoying a friendly conversation. Deb squealed and jumped at Richard. He caught her in mid air and plunked her down on his lap wrapping his arms around her.

"We do have a chair for you Deb," Louise laughed.

"Betchya it's not as comfortable and cushy as my yummy bear's lap," She giggled. Deb gave Richard one loud wet smacking kiss before she jumped off his lap and took her seat.

"Oh Richard isn't this just the ultimate?" she put her hands together and squeezed them against her breasts as she bounced in her seat.

"I was just telling everyone here how wonderful this is and what a perfect theme for my honeybunch." He beamed over at her. "We are very grateful to you all." His eyes did not meet Stella's.

"Stella picked the theme," Deb's lavender eyes watered up again.

"So I heard sweetheart. It's the perfect theme for you." He still couldn't look at her.

The pain of that shot right through Stella. She felt George's arm go around her shoulders offering her his support.

As soon as everyone found their seats, the waiters paraded in carrying trays of food as if on some silent cue and served the first course. The meal went like clockwork. By the looks on everyone's face, the menu choice was bang on.

After the meal was over people got up to mingle while the band set up their equipment on a stage provided for them. When the lights dimmed voices lowered in anticipation of the next phase of the party.

The music was a mixture to please everyone. The dance floor soon filled with people eager to swing and sway and gyrate to show off their dance steps to their favourite tunes.

Although Stella and George along with all her family kept a vigilant watch for any disturbances, ready to take action at a given notice, the evening carried through without the need for it. By the end of the evening they were pleased that Deb could have her day without unwanted trouble, but the strain of being on alert was beginning to show on them all.

George and Stella watched with everyone else as the couple unwrapped their gifts. Deb was heard around the room squealing with delight for each one in turn. After the last gift was opened and Deb's and Richard's combined thanks to everyone, George took Stella to the floor for the last dance. It felt good to be held in his arms and feel the music wash through them as they glided around the dance floor.

"I'm glad your friend had a wonderful party." He whispered in her ear.

"I kept wondering if she would ever run out of tears. They were happy ones, but oh man, they never stopped," she sighed.

"The same could be said about you," he chuckled.

Embarrassed she turned her head on his shoulder. "I can't seem to help it. When she turns on the waterworks mine just seems to follow along."

"You love her." It was a simple statement.

"Yeah, I really do."

The music ended and it was time to say their goodbyes. Hugs and more tears spilled before they took themselves away. Stella was exhausted by the time they reached home.

Turning to George after entering, what she now refers to as their palace, she could not hide the worry behind her eyes.

"Stella, we can't know if he doesn't work on the portal." George offered.

"I know that he's been warned about his activity, but I can't see that stopping him from carrying out his plans. I don't understand why we haven't been able to detect a portal being worked on." She frowned.

"Stella, remember Gobrath is very powerful and very clever. But he won't be able to resist working on the portals for long," he tried to reassure her.

Since they both knew there was nothing more they can do tonight, they decided to turn in and hope the problem will be solved soon. It was a kind of miracle that Stella did not suffer any bad dreams tonight.

TWENTY-ONE

The next morning found Stella struggling to get out of bed. She could not remember ever being so tired before. George was already up and dressed and standing beside the bed with a cup of hot coffee in his hand. The smell of it had her mouth salivating for it.

"Give me some of that and I won't have to kill you," she held out her hand.

"This one is yours. I've already had mine earlier sleepy head." He smiled down at her. Her rumpled hair and drooping eyelids suddenly had lust building in him.

Not able to focus yet she didn't see the look in his eyes. "What time is it?"

"Just after nine o'clock." He set the cup down on the table beside the bed.

"What?" her eyes flew open as she jumped out of bed. "How could you let me sleep so late? What's wrong with you?" She dashed across the room to the bathroom.

"It's so nice to have such a grateful quiet and complacent wife," he mumbled to himself as the blood flowed back up to his brain again. He sighed and decided to wait for her downstairs. "Bet she doesn't even know its Sunday," he muttered to himself.

Showered and dressed and a half a cup of coffee in her, she took herself downstairs. She found George sitting in the library relaxed on one of the sofa's with a book in his hands. He looked up when she entered and put down the book. His eyebrows winged up when he noticed what she was wearing.

"Unless you think we are in imminent danger I don't see the need for you to be wearing your gun this morning."

Stella frowned. "You know I always carry it when I dress for work."

"I had no idea you wanted to go into work today. It is Sunday." He looked baffled.

"Sunday, how did it get to be Sunday?" Now she looked confused.

"Well as a rule it usually follows Saturday on the calendar." He grinned realizing he was right and she had no idea what day it is.

"Don't be a smart ass. I know what day follows which. I just don't know where the days go." She pouted.

"Well in your defense dear, I'd say you have been a bit busy and stretched working so many cases all at once. But now that you know it is Sunday, how about taking the day to relax." He patted the seat next to him.

She did not miss the gleam in his eyes and heat fired up in her center. Saliva began to pool in her mouth just looking at him. Her eyes began to slowly glaze over as lust swelled to fill every fiber in her body.

He watched the needs growing in her causing his own needs to build. As soon as she sat next to him he took her mouth with his and dove in like a thirsty traveler. The taste and scent of her filled his senses to overload. His hands raced to unarm and undress her. Her hands frantically worked to strip away the barriers to feel his skin under her hands.

Heat spread through them both as they rose in the air. Sparks shot out from them, making the room look like the fourth of July. One flick of his fingers had the doors closed and locked. Free of clothing, their hands roamed exploring every inch of each other. They both relished in the sensations of finding and causing muscles to quiver.

Stella grabbed him as he cupped her sending her screaming over the peak. He worked her again before she could come up for air. When she was near the crest he helped her guide him in and with one hard lunge she flew over again. George held his breath and ordered his body not to release. He began a slow rhythm in and out, in and out until he felt her climb once more. She fisted around him, a steamy hot wet velvet vise that almost undid his resolve. Then it was a race to the top as his thrusts grew faster and harder. This time he joined her over the top letting himself go, emptying himself into her. He quivered as she went limp.

They slowly drifted back down to pool on the soft carpet. He slid his sweaty body off hers and lay spent beside her. The only sound in the room was the two of them gasping to fill their lungs with air.

When Stella had the strength to open her eyes, she looked around and was amazed.

"Why didn't the books catch fire?" She gasped out. The walls were lined from floor to ceiling with books.

"I value my library too much. I placed a spell on them." He gasped back. When the feelings returned to his fingers he lifted them, chanted out a short spell and had two tall glasses of cold water appear on the floor beside them.

They sat up and drank like two dying camels and then lay back down again. Once they could feel the rest of their limbs, they gathered up the clothes tossed all around and headed up to the shower.

The rest of the day was spent with both of them trying to entertain the other. Both of them trying to take the other's mind off of the danger that still loomed before them. The more they tried the more edgy Stella got. All day she had the feeling she was missing something.

"You can't be everywhere at once Stella." George knew what was going on in her head.

Her eyes popped wide and she slapped her hand against her head. "Of course, that's it." Her face lit up.

"What's it?" George was confused. It was never easy to keep up with her mind.

"Don't' you see?" She held her hands out. "We need to watch the places we know portals have been activated. The ghosts are watching where one of them spotted the one seen by one of them, the trees are watching the clearing. But we can't have anyone loitering around the Belvedere without being noticed or questioned. Except if that person can't be seen by anyone."

"You're thinking of a ghost," he was catching on.

"Yes," she smiled. "Rita," she called out her friendly ghost's name. But nothing happened. Stella looked concerned at George.

"I don't understand, she always comes immediately when I call her."

"It might have something to do with the protection I've placed around our home Stella. Maybe you need to go outside to call her." George suggested.

That news stunned Stella. She didn't think any spell would work on keeping spirits from going anywhere. She shrugged her shoulders and walked with George to the front door.

Stella called Rita the moment she stepped out the front door.

"The tiny sounds of bells were heard instantly and right behind that sound Rita appeared.

"Ooh, wow great place," she looked around at the exquisite structure of the building. "Hey Stella," she greeted her with a smile.

The eye searing outfit Rita was wearing nearly blinded Stella. She looked like a florescent banana from hat to shoes today. Stella blinked a couple of times to clear her vision.

"Uh, yeah thanks. Rita, I wonder if you could do me a favour."

"Hey we're partners aren't we?" She giggled. The ethereal sound filled the air around them, causing Stella to shiver.

"Uh, sure, yeah right." Stella agreed hesitantly. "Listen I wonder if you could go to the Belvedere in the third ballroom and stay there. If the air shimmers come tell me right away. Rita, I need you to stay there no matter what. Okay?" Stella knew the one thing Rita hated most was boredom.

"Well sure, but can I take a friend to stay with me? Johnathan is a real trouper and we've gotten to be really good friends."

"That's okay, just as long as you don't leave until you hear from me or until you come to tell me you saw the air shimmer. It might take awhile but I need you to stay put until then. Okay?"

"This is like really important huh." Rita's transparent face lit up at the prospects of being in on something important.

"This is hugely important and I'm relying on you to do your part."

"Oh wow, okay Stella. I won't let you down." Rita saluted and poof she was gone.

"Well it sounds like you have all the bases covered that we know about now." George smiled at her when she told him of her conversation.

"I kept thinking I was missing something and then when you said I couldn't be everywhere at once, it clicked in. Thanks." She lifted up onto her toes and pressed her lips to his.

"Glad I could help." George grabbed her before she had a chance to step away and kissed her mouth with more heat sending her head reeling.

There was still no word by the time evening set in. Stella didn't know how much longer her nerves could stand this waiting around. It was a good thing it was the cooks' night off. At least puttering in the kitchen preparing a meal took her mind off of it for a little while.

George knew what this was doing to her, but he could not chance taking her away in case they were needed. If they didn't get word soon, he was afraid her nerves would start to fray. He stood in the kitchen and watched her arrange and prepare the food. At least her mind was busy elsewhere for the time being.

He smiled watching her chop and dice and build sauces. Again he wondered why she never went into cooking for a profession. She certainly had the knack for it. She was simply amazing.

Tonight they sat in the kitchen to eat instead of the formal setting of the dining room. George told her about the women that made up the murder pact. Talking murder and mayhem was a good way to get her to relax.

"You know I still don't get it. According to what you're telling me, Bertrum had no intentions on getting rid of his wife. He was in love with her. Why would she want to kill the golden goose while that goose was still in love with her?"

"From what I gathered from the way she conducted herself in the interview, she developed a passion for killing. Her eyes lit right up when she talked about

Johnathan Foxworth. I believe we stopped a potential murder for hire."

"She got off on killing Johnathan?" Stella's eyebrows winged up.

"Apparently so, we found a lot more on her computer to indicate she was very interested in that kind of life."

"I've always found people are strange," Stella speared a piece of pork put it in her mouth and chewed. "Even in my younger years I noticed the strange workings of the Human minds. I just thought that I was so strange and the fact I didn't fit in with them that I was the oddball. I never knew back then that I was other and simply felt like I didn't fit in anywhere." She frowned. "Now that I know what I do, I still can't wrap my mind around some of the reasons that Humans do what they do to others. It simply boggles the mind. I know that I headed the Homicide Division on the Force and saw so much carnage done by other Humans. At that time I didn't know that I was other, more, and simply accepted it thinking I too was a Human. But now that I know that I am not a Human, it baffles me still." She told him.

They finished their meal talking over all the evidence collected on the case. It seemed to Stella it was going to be a slam dunk for the Crown and that was a good thing, she thought. It was just too bad that they didn't catch them before so many of the husbands were killed. But then the law always tied the police's hands making them follow the rules, whereas criminals didn't have that hindrance. At the time she was on the Force she too had to follow all those rules. The one thing she didn't like was the fact the entire squad followed the same leads like sheep instead of each taking a different lead. That was a huge waste of time and energy. She taught them better than that.

They were just sipping coffee when Graves, the Butler came into the kitchen to announce a visitor. They got up from the counter and went to go to the parlor where Graves had installed him.

"Richard, always a pleasure," George held out his hand walking toward Richard Houston. They shook hands.

Stella noted that Richard wasn't smiling as he took George's hand in greeting. She also noted sadly, that he didn't look at her.

"What brings you here at this hour? Is there something wrong? Is Debra alright?" George queried.

"Deb is fine thank you." His lips stayed firm.

"Please sit down Richard. Is there something I can get for you, a drink, or perhaps some coffee? We were just having a coffee ourselves." George was being the perfect host, but he didn't miss the dislike Richard felt towards his wife.

Richard did sit but he refused the offers of refreshments.

"I think Deb had a good time at the shower," Stella tried to break the ice between them.

"Yes she did and it was very thoughtful of your family to put it on for her," still not making eye contact with her.

"Richard, Stella was part of that as well. I take offense with you ignoring that fact. Now I suggest you tell us what brings you here tonight." George would brook no ill feelings towards Stella in her own home and let him know it.

"I apologize, yes Deb enjoyed it very much thank you Miss. . . Mrs. Smale," he corrected not willing to give up his anger at her.

"Oh, for God's sakes Richard. You don't like me, I get it, and that's fine. But Deb is my dearest and closest friend. I would do anything for her."

Richard jumped up. "No you won't. I asked you to help me to get her to move away from you and your family. She is in danger being this close to you and you both know it." He fumed at them.

"You and I both know that Deb will do whatever she wants and no one can make her do otherwise. She is alive and well and I for one intend to keep her that way so get off my back. Take your prejudices and leave." She spat back.

George took a step to get in between them before fists started flying. "That's enough from the both of you. Richard," he turned to him, "tread carefully while you are inside our home. I will not tolerate your attitude towards my wife. I suggest you tell us the reason for your visit."

"I watched you all at the event last night and I know something is going on. I don't want Deb to be put in the line of danger from whatever it is." He tried staring George down, ignoring his warning.

George sighed. "Yes something is going on but it has nothing to do with Deb, her friends or my family. I am on the police force and something is always going on. Do you dislike me as well because of that?" It was an attempt to get the focus on him and away from Stella.

"I don't need anyone to fight my battles for me," her anger was riding high for both of them now. "All I know Richard, is that if you keep this attitude going towards me you're going to end up being the one that hurts Deb." She tossed back at him. "Now if that's all you came here to say, you can leave. As George just said, we are dealing with bigger problems then your animosity towards me, or inadequacy in protecting your future wife by yourself." She fisted her hands on her hips.

The fire in her eyes and the slap in his face had him take a step back. Not one for physical encounters, he decided to back down. The anger left him feeling drained. He sank down on the sofa and put his head in his hands.

George walked over to the mini bar set in the corner of the room and poured a drink for him. Handing it to him, he put a hand on his shoulder in sympathy for this love struck spineless fool. It must be the artistic gene that made this man into a helpless wimp. George shook his head and stepped back.

Stella was still seething but some part of her felt sympathy for this poor excuse of a man. In her estimation, a man stood until the battle was over. She never did understand what her friend saw in him, but he was the love of her life so she made allowances for him.

Richard finished his brandy and knowing he wasn't going to change Stella's mind to convince Deb to move away, he got up slowly and made his way out. Somehow he knew he was going to have to come to terms of living with danger if he wants to keep Deb in his life.

And, having Stella point out to him his spineless flaw, had his self esteem dwindle even more. Having her shove it into his face the fact that he would never be able to protect Debra, made him think of himself as less than a man. It was a hard pill to swallow and he wondered not for the first time if he was good enough for the love of his life. Maybe it's him that needs to walk away since he can't protect the woman he loves like a man should. He can't understand the reason he can't fight like all other men do. He puts his fighting in the novels he writes, but in real like he simply cannot bring himself to do what the hero's do in his books.

This thought had him in deep thought. He loves Debra with all his heart but he also knows that he is ill equipped to help her in a life-threatening event. Losing her by leaving was less painful than losing her to death. He was never a person to battle or engage in an altercation that could physically harm himself, he simply didn't think he could protect the love of his life, let alone his own life.

Once again Stella was right in shoving in his face that he was not a strong enough man to protect what was most important to him in his life. It grated him to know that Stella is right about him.

TWENTY-TWO

S tella sat in her office the next day drumming her fingers. She would go mad if she just sat around waiting for news of a portal being opened. Her mind was made up. She reached over and pulled the files out of the inbox and set them down in front of her. At least she could keep her mind occupied by going over some of them.

Since the danger was so great, Garrett thought it time to give his daughter some lessons on how to command her gifts. So between going through cases that needed her help and the lessons with her father, the days flew by.

Stella had the transporting pretty much down now. She'd already learned how to communicate with the animal life and vegetation. Garrett was teaching her spell casting. That proved to be more difficult for her. This was more up George's alley than hers, but since she had the blood of both Fairy and Warlock she should be able to do it too.

It was the concentration that was giving her problems. Her mind just wasn't geared to be single minded for long periods. It kept wandering to other things instead of staying focused.

Garrett was overjoyed at the rate she was coming along but not getting the spell casting as well as she took to the other gifts was a bit frustrating for him. He was delighted when she showed him how to bring the sun into his hands. That was one talent he never tried before or knew he even had the talent for.

As days passed Stella found herself becoming more edgy. There was no word yet from the Queen on locating Gobrath. One part of her wished he would never be found so the battle would not take place. On the other hand, she could not stand this waiting around much longer without going completely mad.

Idleness was a real killer for her. And that was a secret she needed to hide from her enemies. Idleness was a huge distraction for her.

Stella had gone through all the files in her inbox and had them marked for the order she would take them on once she was free to do so. When she checked her planner, she found that the 'dragon lady,' was due in a couple of days to go over her accounts. That sent panic racing through her. Her heart began to pound in her chest at the thought of that small woman's imminent visit. She knew she was hyperventilating and a full blown panic attack was close on its heels.

She screamed. She was concentrating so hard on her accountant's impending visit, that when a pair of arms wrapped around her sending shock waves through her, it caused her to scream even harder.

Suddenly the whole room was in a kind of bubble, some sort of protective shield. It was the scent of her father that finally had her relaxing in his grip.

Garrett searched the room with a swift glance around but found no danger lurking. He was confused and relaxed his hold on his daughter. He looked down at his daughter surprised to see her face in full blush, confusing him even more. Garrett raised his eyebrows in question.

"I. . .I was thinking of the 'dragon lady,' sorry." Stella mumbled through her embarrassment.

"Dragon? My darling daughter all the dragons are in the Warlock World. Are you telling me you saw a dragon?" Now it was his turn to panic. If she saw a dragon then a portal has been opened without their knowledge. Gobrath and his father succeeded.

"Not a dragon, Garrett," oh she was mortified. Her face was becoming a deeper shade of crimson by the second. "I was thinking of the 'dragon lady.' It's kind of my pet name I have for my accountant."

"You call your accountant a dragon lady. Well she must be very intimidating to warrant such a title and such a reaction from you." The reason for her embarrassment suddenly became clear to him. Garrett cleared his throat to mask a laugh.

Seeing the amusement in her father's eyes had the blush deepen until it almost matched the colour of her hair. 'Maybe I can conjure up a hole and just sink right into it,' she thought and desperately hoped.

Stella turned her face away, "I know it's silly but I just can't help it. Naomi, that's her name, Naomi Hughes is five foot nothing and looks like Mr. Magoo in her large round black frame thick glasses. She's as plain as dirt and doesn't even try to use enhancements or any attempt at style in her attire. I shouldn't be afraid of her but it's the look and tongue lashing she gives me when she finds I've missed filing away some receipt or other." Stella shivered just thinking of it.

The picture she created in his head had him howling with laughter. Even the pained looked on his daughter's face from his reaction could not hold back the tide of laughter. His sides hurt from it.

God she was pathetic, was all Stella could think. "Oh sure, have a good chuckle, but just remember you've never been the one on the receiving end of that look or one of her severe reprimands."

George walked in at that moment and halted his steps. Seeing his father-in-law bent over howling and his wife standing behind her desk pouting and sporting the reddest face he'd ever seen. Clearly his wife was upset over something and her father found it amusing. What on earth had they been up to, he wondered?

George knew that Garrett had been instructing Stella with her talents. She must have made some kind of mistake that thank goodness didn't seem to have done any damage and he was getting a good laugh over it.

Knowing his wife's temperament, he thought it best he stand near Garrett in case her embarrassment turned to rage. He quietly made his way over to stand next to Garrett and lifted an eyebrow to his wife.

Her humiliation was complete now. All she could do was shrug, "Dragon Lady," was all she said. It was enough to bring a smile to his face. He clued in instantly and fought hard to hold it together.

But at least he didn't have the bad manners to laugh out loud at her, she thought. She was grateful for that at least.

"I see," George was straining hard not to laugh.

Garrett's uncontrollable laughter soon died down and he was wiping away the tears that ran down his face with it. When he could see clearly, he noticed how upset his daughter felt from his actions.

"I am so sorry my dear," he tried for a contrite expression.

"Oh don't worry Garrett, George has the same reaction to my phobia about her," she scowled.

Both men eyed each other and almost made the fatal mistake of bursting out laughing again. It took everything they had to keep their faces straight but the strain was showing in the watery gleam in both their eyes.

"Grrrrrrrr," Stella stomped her foot and whirled on both of them. "So she scares the b-Jesus out of me, so what. You two don't have to deal with her. I'm allowed one phobia and shouldn't have to be criticized for it." Then she stood there raking her hands through her hair.

"It's bad enough that I feel stupid being so frightened of her, now I have to put up with the two of you laughing at me about it. Take your laugh fest and get out." She pointed to the door.

Stella turned and was about to go up the stairs to her private quarters when George grabbed her, twirled her around and firmly kissed her.

Her head started to reel from it when he released her. "I am sorry, darling."

She sighed against him, her anger completely forgotten from the mind spinning kiss. Garrett walked over and ran his hand down the back of her head. "I apologize too sweetheart. It was very rude of me not to be more sympathetic and understanding. Are we forgiven?" He smiled down at her.

Seeing the ridiculousness of the whole situation she relented, forgiving them both. Now that all their emotions were back under control and the deep colour in Stella's face finally receded back to her normal peaches and cream, they sat down and turned the conversation to more important matters.

They finished their coffee and decided it was time to leave when the oval ring of the Queen appeared. The jeweled edge of the oval shot out sparkling lights, a kaleidoscope of colours dazzling the room with them. The Queen appeared in the center of the oval ring. Her jewel studded crown adorned her flaming glory that framed a very worried face.

All three rose up from their chairs and bowed before her.

"My daughter, my sons, I have come to you with news. Ariel has at last given us the information we sought. The news is as bad as we feared I am grieved to say. Gobrath has indeed been creating many portals to both worlds."

"My Queen, has she told you where they are being created?" Garrett asked.

"Yes my son. She told us he has created three to each world and the locations. But we still don't know which one he will open first. I have posted my best and most trusted people to keep watch. I fear that it will not be long before we must take action."

"Mother, what will happen to Ariel?" Stella was concerned for her Queen.

"The penalty for betrayal as you know is death. The counsel has already voted on it and the sentence has been carried out."

Stella saw the pain in her Queen's face for having to put one of her subjects to death. It nearly broke her heart. She knew Ravena must uphold the laws she herself set forth. Ariel had to be sacrificed as a lesson to all her subjects of the seriousness of her actions.

"I am so sorry you had to suffer that mother."

"I have made many difficult decisions in my years of reign my dear, and will make many more. I will always do what I must do to protect my people. My responsibilities are great. Now I must tell you the directions you must search in for the portals to your world."

She did and Stella was not surprised to find they were exactly the three places they already knew about.

"Your Majesty," George spoke up. "Can you tell us how close Gobrath is to completing any of the portals?"

"Alas, my son, at this time I cannot, none of them are being worked on. As soon as my people see one beginning, I will come to you again. That is the best we can do for now. Everything is set up here once we have that information."

"Thank you, Your Majesty," George bowed.

"I fear it will be soon that I call upon you, so be prepared my children and may the Goddess shine on us all." Ravena graced them with one last feeble smile and then vanished. The oval ring melted away.

All three sank back down into their chairs after the queen left them. There was a lot to think about. Now they know it was getting closer to the time when the battle will begin.

Suddenly Garrett and Stella swayed in their chairs grabbing their heads. George jumped up fire balls leapt in his hands ready to be deployed. He frantically scanned the room. He could see nothing to cause what was happening to them. Worried that some invisible force was near, he quickly raised a shield to protect them all.

"Stella, my God, what's wrong? I don't see anything."

Both Garrett and Stella moaned as if in excruciating pain hands squeezing their heads. George felt helpless not knowing what was causing the pain they were suffering or where it was coming from.

Garrett finally managed to whimper as he cradled his head, "the trees. The trees are suffering. They are being burned alive. My God, the pain."

Stella let out a blood curdling scream and fell back in a dead faint. Because of the link between father and daughter, as soon as her mind shut down the pain eased in his own head.

George rushed to Stella but before he got the chance to try to revive her, Garrett slapped his hand over George's arm stopping him. "Leave her be, she is safe and the pain lessens in my head while she is unconscious."

George would have argued, but seeing Stella's chest move up and down slowly showed him she was alright, he turned to Garrett with steel in his eyes.

"We both know that you have greater powers than I, but that will not stop me from causing you as much pain as I am able if you don't tell me what's going on and how to help my wife."

Garrett worked hard to separate the pain going on in his head and the words George was speaking. Finally he managed to look up and saw the determination in George's eyes.

"Somewhere a great forest is being burned down. We, Stella and I, can feel the pain of all those trees.

She has not yet learned to filter her mind. Because hers is completely opened and we are linked, my filter is weakened allowing more of the pain to enter mine. Now that her mind is asleep my filter can work at full capacity again."

"What forest? Where?" George demanded.

"I cannot say, but I don't think it is here. I sense that it is in one of the other worlds. Vegetation is not bound by time or space or dimensions. They are linked in all three worlds."

"Then I suggest you bloody well teach her to filter and do it quickly. From what our Queen just told us, time is running out for all of us." He stormed at Garrett.

"George, take Stella home. I am going to go to the forest and find out what is happening. I will come to your home once that is done and start Stella's lessons on mind filtering."

Garrett did not wait for an answer but vanished, leaving George and Stella alone in her office. George knew that Stella's neighbours saw him enter her building so he did not want to chance anyone entering to find the building empty. He picked up his wife and carried her out of the office and gently placed her inside his car. He locked the doors to her office and climbed in the car and drove them to their home.

Stella surfaced from her feint as he pulled up in their driveway. Her head felt like it wanted to split in half. She placed both hands on her head to keep it from tearing in two and moaned.

Garrett arrived a half hour later. His face was pale and he gratefully accepted a drink George poured for him. Although the pain had eased up some in her head, she sat rocking herself on the sofa still suffering from what was left. She looked over at her father with pained eyes.

George waited, frustrated at not being able to help either of them. This was beyond his powers and he felt useless. All he wanted was to take the pain from Stella and knew that he couldn't.

After taking a sip, Garrett cupped the glass between his hands. He looked over at his daughter and was glad that he could ease the pain she was suffering. When he looked up at George, he saw the frustration pouring from him.

"It comes from the Warlock World. Apparently one of the Wizards there was in a forest casting spells and one went horribly wrong. The Wizard's spell backfired and it set him on fire which quickly spread to the forest he was in. A large area caught fire and burned down."

Garrett looked back at his daughter. "Stella I have to teach you to filter your mind. Once the battle takes place you will have to be focused and not have something like this cause you any distractions. Gavin will need the both of us to work with him totally focused."

"The pain, the suffering, oh father, I just couldn't take it. I felt everything the trees did. It was like I was being eaten alive with the fire too. I'm sorry." Tears slid down her cheeks, her mind still fresh with the memories of what the trees felt.

"I know my daughter. I feel it each time there is a great forest fire here on earth. That is why I must teach you how to put up a filter in your mind. There is a good side and a bad side to the powers we possess my dear."

Now that George knew the pain his wife suffered had nothing to do with Gobrath, he left the two alone to get on with Stella's lessons. He hoped and prayed that she will learn this one quickly. Never did he ever want to see her suffer like that again.

Stella had never worked so hard on anything else as she did on the filtering lessons. She had one great incentive; she did not think she could ever survive such horrific pain again. She not only felt their pain, but it felt as though her own body was being consumed by the fiery blasts of flames. They worked at it until after midnight when Garrett was finally convinced that she could master erecting the filter in her mind at will.

It must have been in their blood, some inner sense that came with the magic. They both awoke with a sense that today would have them fighting for their very lives. They tried to act like this was just like any other normal day. They went through the morning ritual of showering and eating breakfast. But the strain was too much and they dropped all pretenses after awhile. The only good thing about this day was that it was Saturday and neither one had to go into work.

It was the same for all of those at the Blake Manor. They were all on edge. Even Gwen felt it when she woke up and drove over to her mother's to wait it out. Garrett felt it would be better if Stella was with him when the Queen announces the location of the portal. He called her to have her and George come over.

It would have been comical had it not been for the fact it was deadly serious. Everyone in the Manor was tripping over each other trying to be polite in an attempt to soothe each other. Nerves were frayed to the maximum by the time early evening set in.

Two things happened at once. Stella and Garrett heard the tinkling of little bells and an oval ring appeared. Nerves already taught, Stella let out a scream knowing Rita was close. She must be outside the Manor. There was no mistaking the sound of those bells Rita wore around her neck and dangling from her ears. Then she remembered that Rita told her once that she was surprised to find she could not enter the Blake Manor.

"My daughter, what has startled you? Is there danger where you are?" Ravena's concern was so touching to Stella.

"No mother, I'm sorry. It's just that you came to us at the same time as a ghost friend. She cannot enter here for some reason. I had her watching one of the locations for us."

"I see," Ravena's expression did not change. She looked very concerned. "We have found a portal being activated. It is in the Northwest. We need you all there immediately." She vanished without another word.

"Maria get word to the Coven right away and tell them the portal is being opened at the Belvedere. They know what to do." Stella yelled as they all ran for the door.

Maria pulled out her wand and cast her spell as she ran with them.

Rita was shocked as all the Blake family ran out the door.

"We know, the Belvedere," Stella called out to Rita. They all waited for Maria to finish her spell before joining hands in a circle and vanished.

Rita looked at Johnathan who was clearly baffled by all this and smiled. "Let's go watch the fun," she said and took his hand and vanished too.

Within seconds they all reappeared in the middle of the third floor ballroom. George quickly put up a shield to make the entrances to that room disappear. No one in the hotel would be able to find it until they were done. Then he cast a spell that would make the room sound proof. The rest, he knew would be up to his wife and father-in-law and the Witches.

Part of the Coven arrived only seconds after they did. They raised their wands and cast a spell to keep the portal from being closed. The rest of the Coven split up to be at the other two locations casting spells to seal them so they could not open. The spells were given to them by George who was given them by Gareg. This was the crucial part they were needed for.

Stella and Garrett heard the bells but paid no attention to them. Rita and Johnathan stood close to where the door to the room once was and waited too. Everyone was poised and staring at the point in the room where the air shimmered. The only sound in the room was the constant chanting from all the Witches to keep the portal from closing.

The shimmering spread out and suddenly they were face to face with Gobrath. The look of total surprise on his face would have been comical at any other time, but the danger facing them had all of them focused completely on the job at hand.

A quick glance told them that Ravena, Gareg and Gavin had not arrived yet. Gobrath recovered from his shock quickly and soon fireballs were being fired at them from where he stood. The Witches knew they could not stop their chanting spell and continued relying on the others to protect them.

George immediately went to them and cast a shield around them for protection as he threw fireball for fireball. Stella and Garrett stood side by side as they transformed. They floated like two large Greek Gods before Gobrath. He had never seen the likes of this apparition standing on the other side of the portal. As he fought, his mind tried to shake off the shock of such a vision. He did not possess this kind of power.

Total anger took over him at seeing something he did not have and wanting it badly. He aimed for the Witches that prevented him from closing the portal. Now seeing his attempts bounce off a shield he concentrated on the two huge entities. Here too his efforts could not penetrate. So engulfed with rage at not being able to slay these people, he jumped through the portal, flames shooting from him.

Stella and Garrett hurled lightning bolts at him. They bounced off at first, but Garrett could see Gobrath's protective shield was weakening. They tried to bind him, but somehow Gobrath had found a way to stop that spell from affecting him.

Gobrath glanced around the strange room he found himself in. The room began to shake beneath the other's feet and it filled with the stench of smoke from the lightning bolts and fireballs. The Witches kept chanting as though their very lives depended on it and it did. Sweat beaded on their brows as the portal kept trying to close behind Gobrath. Stella and Garrett kept trying to bind him. They knew they needed Gavin to add to their strength or all would be lost.

Gobrath's shield was weakening further as the battle continued. The constant pelting against it was weakening it but Gobrath was giving as much as he was getting. If the Queen did not show soon the battle could turn either way.

Watching Gobrath's powers grow had Stella desperate enough to stop chanting the binding spell long enough to bring the sun into her hands.

Taking her assistance even for that short time from her father had Gobrath's fireball that he aimed at him hit his mark. Garrett reeled from it almost losing the power to keep his transformation up. She cast the pieces of sun at Gobrath and his shield evaporated.

George's fireballs hit their mark and had Gobrath backing up towards the portal. Suddenly unprotected, Gobrath feared for his life making his aim to waver and miss hitting his targets.

Gobrath cursed and swore at the strange beings that dared to attack him. In his mind there should be no beings stronger than himself. He is the prince of the Warlock World. Warlocks are the most powerful magical beings alive. These strangers should be quaking in their boots instead of daring to defy and attack him. What kind of World is this if none here quaked at the very sight of him?

He had never felt fear before in his life. In his mind it did not matter that there were such strange beings as the two huge entities floating above everyone. What really shocked him was the fact that the Witches were not frightened of him or willing to bow down to him. They too should fear him. Witches have always feared and obeyed Warlocks. They are the lowest in the chain of power and have always known their place. But now that his shield was gone, he knew he had to get back to his world and think over what he just witnessed, the sights and actions of those in this strange World. Never has he ever had anyone not only stand up to him, but to have the audacity to actually feel justified in battling with him, against him. This is unbelievable.

Gobrath managed to jump back into the Fairy World. The efforts of Stella and Garrett had given Ravena, Gareg and Gavin enough time to get to the portal. They appeared behind him as he stepped back into it.

There was no time to lose. Stella, Gavin and Garrett joined in a chant that would bind him hopefully long enough for Ravena and Gareg to cast the spell of forgetfulness. This time it took the combined effort of the three of them to have the golden ropes appear and wind around him. The moment the bindings appeared and remained they heard a God awful scream from Gobrath. That sound vibrated all the way through the portal to their side of it, shaking the floor beneath them. But they all stood firm and never wavered their concentration for an instant. Stella and Garrett concentrated on their binding spell as the Witches kept up the chant to hold the portal open. But they were all tiring from their efforts.

They saw the strain of casting the spell was hard on Gavin but he did not sway in his attempts. His green eyes narrowed and sweat beaded his brow but he kept chanting until the ropes appeared and wrapped around Gobrath. Stella and Ravena and Gareg were all so proud of him.

They all heard the royal couple chanting and watched as they lifted their arms high. The air shimmered around Gobrath and he slunk down to the ground, arms forced to his sides, kneeling and helpless.

Ravena peered through the portal, her face pale and drawn. She nodded her head indicating that the spell was in place and working. Gobrath should never again find a way to open a portal. All the spells he used were gone from his mind forever.

Stella and her father bowed to her and then she turned to the Witches still chanting.

"You can stop chanting the spell. Gobrath is bound and our Worlds are safe. Thank you all so much for your help. None of this would be possible without it. Please thank the rest of your Coven for us."

Once they were dismissed, the portal closed and without a word, the Witches quickly transported back to their Coven. Some of them did not like being this close to members of the Fairy bloodline.

Stella and her father released the heat and changed back, floating gently down to the floor. George went to his wife immediately wrapping his arms around her. It surprised him to find she did not sink down from the transformations but was strong and steady on her feet.

Taking a few minutes to get their breath back from all their efforts and the terrors of the battle and what could have been if they had not succeeded, they gathered in a circle. Stella tied her hair back and smiled at her father.

"I'm sorry I left you alone for a second but I just felt I had to do something to distract him. My God he is powerful, I could feel it. I've never felt such power before. As powerful as we both are, he is even more so. But I also felt the dark in him."

"Your sun cast took away his shield. I think he will be thinking of that for a very long time." Garrett laughed. "And yes, he is the son of King Gorkin, an original Warlock. His powers are far greater than ours but somehow I don't think he is gifted with that particular talent.

Knowing what could have been had things gone the other way had all the women a bit giddy, all, that is, except Maria. She knew this was going to be the breaking point for many in the Coven and her heart broke for them.

George lifted the spell he cast on the room and they joined hands to transport back to the Manor.

For the first time in Rita's afterlife, she was struck dumb. It was the most incredible thing she had ever witnessed and even she could admit she'd never want anything like that to happen again. All the fear and tension in the room had her frightened. She grabbed Johnathan's hand and disappeared to go tell all her friends.

Back in the Manor, gathered once more around the kitchen table, everyone sighed with relief. They were all tired and pale from the strain of the battle.

The women all talked about the boy and how beautiful and brave he is, while Stella, George and Garrett talked about the battle.

"Had you not thought fast and found a way to destroy his shield, things could have turned out differently. I'm so proud of you my daughter," Garrett hugged Stella.

"I'm of two minds on that one Garrett. She put both of you at risk when she disconnected with you." George could not help the anger he felt from the fear of thinking she could have died in her attempts.

"George you saw his shield weaken but still he was strong. Something had to be done and quickly. I know," she put up a hand to stop him from arguing with her, "it was a risk and it left Garrett vulnerable for a few seconds. But I knew I had to do it."

"Your instincts proved right," Garrett stood up for his daughter. "George, instincts are part of her gifts too and so far they have never failed her or proved her wrong. Gobrath had to be completely vulnerable for the binding to work."

"I can't help it Garrett, I don't like it when Stella puts herself in harms' way. I can't bear the thought of losing her." Pain filled his eyes.

"George," Stella laid her hand on his cheek, "we are what we are. Had I not done it we all could have died tonight. I feel the same way about you too. There are times I fear for you too, but I must accept what you are and trust you enough to know you will be safe. I'm only asking you to do the same with me."

"I'm used to being the one with the most power and the one to protect you. That is not the case anymore. Don't misunderstand me darling, I'm proud of who you are and what you have become. I do trust you my darling, but that does not mean I will stop worrying about you. It's hard for me to know that you don't need my protection anymore, that you are stronger than me. Warlocks have always been stronger than Fairies and Elves." He leaned closer to her and gently kissed her lips. "You are everything to me."

She also knew that as her new powers grow and she can take care of herself that this is hurting George's pride and his male ego. This is going to be so hard for him to adjust to, if he can adjust to it. God, she hopes he can.

Stella felt the struggle going on inside him and her heart filled with pain at knowing they can't go back to the way they were before.

Exhausted and happy that everything turned out well, they left the Manor to go home. To go back to a normal life now that they knew there will be many, many tomorrows in their World.

Both Stella and George knew that after tonight things will change. Their love will always be strong and grow, but their roles in each other's life were about to change. Stella didn't know how to take this and George was worried that he will not be useful to her from now on like he had been up until this point. She was proving to be stronger than him and he has to find a way to deal with this change.

For a Warlock to lose the ranking of power is something that can't be taken lightly and needs time to adjust, if that is at all possible. As in the Humans, Warlocks have egos and once that ego is damaged, a man, human or Warlock, must find a way to deal with that. For a Warlock, it is more difficult. Power is everything to Warlocks. It is their strength and basic foundation. It is essentially who and what they are.

For Stella, her mind was filled with all the new powers and gifts that have come to her in such a short time. She didn't know if she is strong enough to deal with them. After what happened tonight she didn't know if she can control them or even wanted them. Tonight scared her in more ways than her mind can cope with at the moment. Her gut was screaming at her that this is only the beginning and that too scared her. She didn't want to think about what was coming and what she was becoming as well.

Her biggest worry is losing George over this extra power she has. That caused a pain greater than the forest burning down. She knew they have to find a way to deal with this change. Living without George simply is not an option for her. Stella put all her hopes on the love they have for each other. Surviving this latest danger gave her hope that together they will always handle whatever comes at them. They will both find a way to adjust. They must find a way.

This battle cost more than anyone could ever imagine. Should there be more battles in the future; Stella hopes that George will be there by her side to fight alongside her. To lose him will be to lose everything. Stella knows that time will tell if she is to go back to being alone or have the man that fills her heart willing to stay by her side. Deep inside Stella knows they won a battle but her instincts told her there is still a war to win.

Printed in the United States
By Bookmasters